Slumming it on...
Slut Street

Slumming it on...

Slut Street

A Randi Michaels Novel

Dalia Lance

4 Horsemen
Publications, Inc.

4 Horsemen
Publications, Inc.

Published By: 4 Horsemen Publications, Inc.

4 Horsemen Publications, Inc.
PO Box 417
Sylva, NC 28779
4horsemenpublications.com
info@4horsemenpublications.com

Cover & Typesetting by Valerie Willis
Edited by Tilda M. Cooke

Paperback ISBN-13: 978-1-64450-035-4
Hardcover ISBN-13: 979-8-8232-0706-5
Audiobook ISBN-13: 978-1-64450-033-0
Ebook ISBN-13: 978-1-64450-034-7

DEDICATION

To my real life Alex: Thanks for keeping me sane.

Acknowledgments

Finishing book two of this series has been an interesting ride. I want to thank some people without whom this would not have been accomplished:

To Dem Bitches, you have made me smile throughout this COVID time when I could only see you though a zoom call. Thank you for inspiring Randi's best friends.

To Vanessa, you have been an amazing light. You have so much to give and I cannot wait till I see your book on the shelf next to mine.

To Val, this year has been ridiculous and more epic then I could have imagined. Thank you for being the publishing yin to my yang. You inspire me.

For every superhero there is a sidekick. I can't believe we are going on twenty years. I am not sure I could have done this writing adventure with anyone else.

Hey B, thanks for always making sure I remember that I can do anything I decide to. And for always cheering me on along the way.

To Justin and Jeni, you are truly amazing and thank you for making me proud every day of my life. You might be my greatest accomplishment.

Finally, to Jonathan, thank you for always pushing me towards my dreams and standing by me, even when I am typing away for hours and hours. Your love is amazing. Times.

TABLE OF CONTENTS

1

DATING IS A
VERY BAD WORD

"You can't eat where you have sex!" Alex exclaimed from across the table.

I looked down at my latte as I considered how this conversation was going. Not well at all. In fact, I wasn't actually sure if I ever thought this could go well. Trying to explain to Alex that I was thinking about having a real relationship was always going to be a challenge. A large part of me knew she wouldn't think it was a good idea.

"But this is different..." Even as the words left my mouth, I knew I was full of shit. Alex was right. The latest man in my series of playmates was not what I should be looking at for anything more than that. It was absolutely not the right place or time for a relationship.

You may be wondering why this conversation was happening. If you didn't travel to My Home on Whore Island with me, you most likely need the Cliff-Notes to get caught up. If you did visit the Island with me, you can skip ahead a couple of pages.

My name is Randi Michaels and I don't "date."

To be more accurate, I don't date *anymore*. I have found that I am much better when I am spending time with what I call "playmates."

My last actual relationship ended because he cheated on me. Of course, this led, in a very stereotypical fashion, to him breaking my heart. I decided that I didn't need a relationship or even the first name of a playmate to be happy. Honestly, I have been quite happy on several occasions, but in the last few months, I have had found that I violated my own rules about getting attached to a playmate. These violations have led me to sitting across from one of the most amazing and yet least forgiving people in my life: Alex.

We all, hopefully, have that person in our lives that keeps us grounded. Alex is that for me. One of our routines is heading to our local bookstore/coffee shop. This place affords us yummy lattes and interesting people watching opportunities. However, on this fateful afternoon, I was the only person Alex had fixated her attention on. I didn't like it.

You may be wondering why.

One of the key parts to a truly real "Friends with Benefits" type of arrangement is that you are not actually *dating* that person.

What is the line that separates this? I think most people would define dating as having an interest in continuing that relationship for longer than say twenty-five minutes in the bathroom stall of a local dance club. That is, of course, a story for another time (Check out chapter seven 😊).

Dating though, for the most part, seems to have something other than a purely sexual connotation, meaning there are some kind of feelings associated with that person.

I think that Urban Dictionary said it best: "When a man/woman goes out with another individual or many different people to configure compatibility; not having any clear commitment; it may be as short as a week or for many years. *It is not a relationship*."

That is the key, isn't it? Dating is not a relationship. It is also not simply sexual. This is because you are trying to find to figure out compatibility. When you are simply sexual, the only compatibility you are discovering is mostly physical.

"*You* are not supposed to *date* them!" I could tell she had been thinking on this for some time. "These were your rules, and now you seem to be chucking them out the window in favor of a pile of bad choices."

She was pissed off.

She was also, painfully, right.

> *Whore Tip: Never back down from rules you set for yourself unless you decide that the rule was not correct in the first place or possibly no longer applies. Basically, don't do things for others that have an opportunity to hurt you in some way in the process.*

> (In case you were not on Whore Island when I started this adventure, I will offer up small bits of wisdom I get on my journey as *Whore Tips*. You never know when you could use a little nugget of Randi brilliance.)

Alex stared hard at me as she took another sip of her latte. I wanted to justify my reasoning, but I knew she was correct. I wanted to scream that this was my life and she had no right to tell me who I could and could not see.

There was a little voice in my head, however, that told me again how right she was. I knew when I explained how Blake—using his real name, no cute nickname to refer to him—wanted to take me to dinner. Of course, I had eaten dinner with some of my playmates. But Blake was courting me. He wanted to "take me to dinner." I found that after a year of not dating anyone, some hidden part of me wanted to have someone want to actually date me for real.

"Is this about Jessie again?" Alex softened her tone. When she said his name, I flinched. It still hurt a little more than it should have.

"No. Of course not." Again, as the words left my mouth, I knew I was lying.

In order to understand fully what happened that brought us to this moment, I am going to have to take you back a bit. Four months actually.

2

THE CABIN IN THE WOODS

J essie was nothing short of a perfect playmate. He was 6'2, blonde hair cut short, blue eyes and muscles for miles. He was also a soldier for hire. I know it sounds very spy novel-like, but the job does exist out there, and I happened to nab one of them on the beach one night. This meant that he was only around every now and then. A perfect arrangement.

He would show up in town, we would have sex for days, and then he would be gone to parts unknown.

> *Whore Tip: If you find the perfect arrangement, don't mess with it. It is in most people's nature to desire to know the details. Sometimes not knowing can be even better.*

He wouldn't text or call unless he was in town and ready to play. Occasionally, I would receive an email from a random address that would always contain our code word "Watusi." In case you are wondering, a Watusi is a cow with exceedingly long horns. He told me one night about the first time he saw a group of them when he was on a job and the sheer size of their horns had scared him. This of course led to endless teasing from me about the big bad soldier being afraid of a cute spotted cow.

It had been months since I had last heard from Jessie. I was just driving home from a crazy work week. That means I spent most of it not having enough time for the million meetings (more than half of which could have been handled in a well-worded email).

As I sat in traffic on the way home, I realized I had been so caught up in work I hadn't planned what I was doing with three days off. We had hit a huge target as a company, and the boss man had promised me the extra day off. I was almost home, contemplating the empty days ahead, when the

phone rang.

I looked at the caller ID. It was a number I did not recognize. I usually did not answer these types of calls. But with a very lazy weekend ahead, I thought it might lead to one of those terribly fun adventures or maybe just a telemarketer. You have to live a little, right?

"Hello?"

"Hey Baby," I heard a voice say.

"Who is this?" I asked. It flashed through my mind for a moment that I should not have so many guys calling me by pet names that I would have to ask for a name. Then I remembered that I use nicknames to remember them.

"Who do you think it is?" I recognized his voice now, deep and inviting. My heart began to beat faster. I still remembered how he smelled and tasted—God I missed that.

"Oh, hey." This is all I managed to say. I was a total dork. He seemed to have the ability to make me feel like a schoolgirl with a huge crush.

> *Whore Tip: Remember that we are all human.*
> *Crushes happen. It is what you do with them*
> *that matters.*

"What are you doing this weekend?" he asked.

I wanted to say something witty or coy. I would have even set-tled for "cute." Since I couldn't think of anything that fit the bill, I turned to more practical thinking like: *Should I sound busy? Should I play hard to get?* I didn't ever want to sound desperate; it threw off the dynamics when that happened. About a million things raced through my mind and until he finally said, "Are you there?"

I wasn't talking. This was bad. "I'm here. Just thinking." That was not the best cover but at least the words came out in some sensible order. It was amazing the effect he could have on me. I pulled into my driveway, slipping the car into park and focusing on my phone.

"So...are you busy this weekend?" he asked again.

"Not really. Why? What's up?" Any upper hand I was attempting to have faded away, but at least I was starting to sound less like a teenager now, or so I hoped. I walked up to my porch, fumbling through my keys to find the one that would open the door. I had just held the correct key up to the lock when he said in a playful voice, "I am picking you up in two hours. I have a surprise for the weekend."

"Okay, where are we going?" I asked, wondering if this was really happening.

"It is going to be cold," he warned. "See you at 8!" With that, he hung up.

I stood at my front door for a minute, taking in what just hap-pened. I then caught a glimpse of my hair in the window of the door all windblown from having the windows open on the way home, and it occurred to me that I had only two hours to get ready for this, whatever "this" was.

I ran inside and decided to shower first. As I pulled my clothes off and started the water running, I remembered the last time we saw each other. We stayed up all night moving from bar to bar, dancing and drinking the night away. We ended up in an alley unable to keep our hands off each other for another moment. He lifted me up and pushed me against a wall. Sliding my panties to the side, he slid his hard cock inside of me.

It had only taken a few minutes, but it was the most primal moment of my life. He then told me he had to leave within a few hours. We both called separate rides, and when I was about to get into mine, he grabbed me and kissed me. He kissed me as if he were burning the taste and feel of me into his brain.

I felt him on my lips for days after. I still remembered the warmth of his lips, the feel of his tongue as it moved with mine. He tasted so good. I could still feel his arms around me, how he pressed himself against me.

A shiver ran down my entire body, and my nipples hardened. I felt a new warmth between my legs, and I leaned back in the shower, lingering, feeling the warm water run through my hair and down my body. I stood directly under the shower head, turning the hot water up so that the warmth was almost too much to take. I let my fingers play down my face, across my lips, down my chest. At the thought of his mouth on mine, a small moan escaped my lips and my fingers moved down my stomach, but my phone rang again, snapping me out of my fantasy. I raced out of the shower, grabbed a towel, and almost ran over my cat. Henry jumped up from his spot right outside the bathroom door, glaring at me as he moved away from where he had been impatiently waiting for me to finish.

I took a deep breath, and after a momentary pause to compose myself, I answered the phone. "Hey," I said in the cutest voice I could muster.

"Did you send Dad his present?" It was my sister. I reminded myself why I had caller ID. I answered her as quickly as I could and hung up the phone.

Grabbing the bag I used for small trips out of the closet, I packed everything I could think of for chilly weather. I even included two sweaters and my jacket. Living in Florida, I almost never found a use for these items.

I pulled on my jeans, tank top, and flip flops, then went and grabbed my toothbrush. *I might be overpacking. He didn't say how long we would be gone.* I thought about calling him, but decided that would take away the surprise.

When the doorbell rang, I grabbed my bag, purse, and jacket. I opened the door. He was standing there in jeans and a blue t-shirt. He smiled and pulled me to him. Leaning down slightly, he placed his lips against mine. I closed my eyes. His lips were strong and yet soft at the same time. His tongue slid into my mouth; I moaned slightly, and his kiss became deeper as I felt his desire for me as well. I used my lips to pull his tongue into my mouth deeper and then slid it out almost to the tip. I moved down it again and then released.

I opened my eyes again, looking into his. "Miss me?" he whispered. I gently bit my lip and nodded. His eyes were blue like a perfect spring day. I could get lost in them. Still holding me close, he smiled and said, "Ready?" I knew he had no idea how ready I was for him. "Yep" was all I could say as he kissed me again lightly and grabbed my bag out of my hand.

We walked over to his truck, he opened the back, and he deposited my bag inside. He then came around and opened the door for me. I climbed in and buckled my seatbelt as he closed the door and walked around the front to get in the driver's side.

As he closed his door, he picked up what looked like a bandana from the steering wheel. He smirked and motioned for me to lean in closer. "Close your eyes," he said. I smiled. He was so cute. He wrapped the blindfold around my eyes. I could feel his breath on my face. "No peeking," he said and kissed me lightly on my nose.

I heard him start up the car, and we began driving. It became more exhilarating as I sat there not being able to see. It was a surprise, and he had planned it, which alone made it amazing.

We talked for a while, laughed, and smiled. He had amazing stories, and I told him of my recent adventures. He always had a way of making me smile. I realized we had been driving for several hours, and it was getting late. He still did not say anything about where we were headed.

I yawned a little, trying to hide it by turning my head. His fingers touch my cheek, warm lines being drawn by them. "Are you tired, baby?" he asked me.

I nodded. "A little." I felt a blanket placed over me.

"Sleep for a little while then. We will be there soon." His fingers ran down my face to my neck, and then I felt his fingers through my hair. I curled up as best I could in the seat, wrapping the blanket around me. He continued to play with my hair as I drifted off into sleep.

Some amount of time later, I felt the car slow down and come to a stop. As I woke up, I realized the blindfold was still on. I heard his door open and close, and a gust of frigid air came through. I sat there for several minutes in silence. I pulled the blanket closer around me. Then my door opened, and I smiled and looked in that direction. He leaned in and picked me up out of the car. I wrapped my arm around his neck. It was cold as the wind hit my arm and face. I buried my face in his chest trying to block the cold as I heard his footsteps as he was walking. I recognized the sound as the crunching of snow.

He walked up three steps, and then I felt him push open a door with his shoulder. He walked a few more steps and set me down on a surface covered by pillows. I was warm, and I heard the sound of a crackling fire. Then I heard him shut the door.

He came back and sat beside me, leaning in to kiss me again. He pulled back and whispered into my ear, "Do you have any idea where you are?"

I smiled and licked my lips slightly "No, but it is cold."

He laughed, then pulled the blindfold from my face. As my eyes adjusted to the light, I saw we were in a cabin, and I was sitting on a very plush couch. It was dark outside, but the fire in the fireplace was the only source of light besides two candles on the small table on the side of the couch. I could see the moon shining on the snow through the window.

I took his face in my hands and pulled him close to me. "Thank you," I whispered, looking into his eyes and stroking his face with my fingers. He closed his eyes. I traced the lines of his face. "You must be tired," I said with a wink.

He smiled and pulled the blanket from around me while shaking his head no. I felt my heart begin to race again.

I leaned back, watching him as he stood up, removed his jacket, and slid his shoes off. I stood, slid off my flip flops, and let them fall to the floor. Walking up, I slid my arms around his waist and pressed my lips against his neck, kissing and tasting his skin as I pulled off his shirt and tossed it to the floor. I ran my fingernails down his back and then his chest, lightly licking his shoulders. His skin was smooth, and I could taste the saltiness of his sweat.

Wrapping his arms around my waist, he kissed my neck as I moved slowly around in a circle, so his back faced the couch. I moaned as I felt his teeth against the skin of my neck. Pushing him down on the couch, I crawled on top of him, straddling his waist. Looking down at him, I smiled and asked, "Are you sure you're not tired?"

All he did was wink as he slid his fingers through my hair, bringing my face to his. He kissed me deeply as I began to moan again. Feeling his tongue dance with mine, I pushed my hips to him, grinding against the solid length of him. I enjoyed how hard he already was underneath his jeans. I moved my hips, rocking back and forth, as I kissed him harder. My core rubbed against the fabric of my jeans. I was getting wet, and then my legs began to quiver, warmth passing through me as I came hard, back arching as I dug my nails into his chest. I moaned so loudly it was almost a scream. This was just the beginning.

His hands were at my waist again pulling off my shirt. His fingers deftly unhooked the clasp of my bra and pulled it down my shoulders. My nipples hardened as he clasped them in each hand and began to rub slightly. Moans escaped my lips as I moved my hips again on top of him. He pulled each nipple with fingers tugging slightly, my nails digging into his chest again as he played with them, his fingers caressing and toying. Flipping my head back, I came again hard on top of him. He knew how to please me.

Leaning down to kiss him, I shivered as his hands moved down my back. I kissed down his neck, gently biting him. Moving down his chest, I took each of his nipples into my mouth, moving my tongue around them, sucking slightly as I felt him move beneath me. I kissed his stomach lightly, little butterfly kisses, letting my nails follow down his chest and stomach. I let my mouth caress him through the jeans, my warm breath a tease as I undid the button and unzipped the fly. Pulling them open, I kissed his exposed hips and thighs, letting my lips get so close to his cock that he could feel my breath. I pulled his jeans off, kissing down each leg before letting them fall to the floor. I stood there looking down at him as I undid my own jeans and slid them to the floor. I pulled off my panties and dropped them on the pile of clothes now formed on the floor.

I looked at him, watching as the firelight danced across his skin, letting my eyes wander to how hard his cock was. God, I wanted to feel him inside of me. I crawled up between his legs again like a cat seeking a saucer of milk.

> *Whore Tip: Always be willing to go after what you want. You will be amazed at how turned on your partner will be by your boldness.*

I began by licking his inner thigh, letting my tongue slide up the entire length of his shaft. Sliding the head of his cock into my mouth, I tasted him, loving how he throbbed against my tongue.

Circling once more around the tip, I released him, sat up, and slid my legs on either side of his hips, holding him with my hands I slid him into me slowly.

His hard length filled me completely. My warm wetness surrounding him, I began to slide slowly up and down his cock, moving my hips forward and back taking him all the way inside of me. He placed his hands on my hips urging me to go faster, and I tightened around him as I came again, moaning as I pushed even faster into him, feeling my clit rub against his skin. I looked down to see him watching me, taking in my face as I came again on top of him. His gaze made my legs quiver again, and my moans were almost screams as I orgasmed over and over.

He swelled inside of me, and he pulled me to him as he pushed deeper inside. His hands slid up my back, bringing my lips to his, and his tongue slid between my lips as he came inside of me. I heard his moans as he released deep and hard.

I lay there on top of him, listening to him breathe. His cock was still pulsing from the orgasm. His fingertips trailed down my back in large circular sweeps sending tingles down my spine. I sat up again looking down at him. He was smiling.

Lying down next to him, he pulled the blanket over us. I put my head on his chest and ran my fingers through his hair, down his neck and chest until I his breath became steady and I could tell he was asleep. I looked up at him one last time, blew out the candles, placed my head on his chest again, and fell asleep in his arms.

This was of course one of the sexiest times of perfect fantasy. A part of me felt like all my adventures had led up to this moment.

Whore Tip: Enjoy the perfect moments. I hope you have many of them.

3

Someone Else is "Jessie's Girl"

I n the morning, I woke up to the smell of coffee. He brought me a cup of black coffee without creamer. Unfortunately, I need a little cream in my coffee. It is interesting when people do those little gestures that get lost because they didn't pull it off completely the way you wanted it.

> *Whore Tip: Remember to judge a nice gesture for the intent and not always execution. That doesn't mean you can't enlighten the person to what you like or desire. Just use a bit of tact.*

I got up and grabbed my shirt and undies from my bag, sliding them on as I used the bathroom. I had forgotten to bring by toothbrush with me, so I decided to fix the coffee first before rounding that up. I walked into the kitchen and Jessie was sitting at the table looking out into the snow.

"Hey Babe, where did you find this place?" I asked as I opened the fridge to find it empty. No milk. No food. I was hoping he had thought of more than last night as far as this weekend. I could be distracted by his yumminess, but eventually, I would want to eat something. I sighed a little, closing the door, and moved to sit across from him. As I took a sip of my coffee, I reached out my other hand toward his, but he pulled it away and turned to look out the window again.

"Hey Watusi, what's on your brain?" I asked, using the most playful voice I could muster. He sighed heavily. Immediately, I began to wonder what I had done. It's terrible that people look inward first. At least I do.

He stood up and walked over to lean on the counter. I could tell he was putting distance between us. He cleared his throat and then finally said, "God. This is hard."

"What's hard?" I needed whatever this was to go faster. Waiting for clearly unwelcome news like this didn't work for me. We used condoms so I was quite sure this could not be an STI (sexually transmitted infection) conversation. I played out a bunch of scenarios, but that never helps anything.

> *Whore Tip: Try not to fill the vacuum usually created by lack of information. You can end up sucked into that black hole as well.*

Jessie finally looked up and his face was almost pale. "I'm... Randi, I am married."

I dropped my coffee.

"Listen, I know I lied," he started. I knew I didn't want him to finish.

"Take me home," I said standing up to avoid the mess I had created by dropping the coffee and the cup on the floor.

I moved toward the bathroom again. I could hear he was following, but my heart was pounding so hard in my chest that I felt like I was going to throw up. We had been fucking for almost a year.

When you are in a confined place, you discover quite quickly that there is not an easy spot to be "alone." The bathroom was not where I wanted to be, but it was my only option. After several minutes, Jessie stopped pounding on the door and trying to explain. I couldn't understand the words he said anyway. I was in shock.

I sat on the toilet with the lid closed trying to put together everything that I had just heard. Jessie was married.

> *Whore Tip: Always, always, always give yourself time to think about a situation when you can. Your first reaction may not always be the right one, even if you think it is in the moment.*

While sitting there formulating what I wanted to say to him, figuring out the questions I wanted to ask, I realized something: I wasn't crying because I wasn't sad. After having been cheated on in my last *real* relationship, I had started to truly understand my emotions.

My rule clearly said that I did not mess with anyone in any kind of monogamous relationship, especially if they were married. Since I knew firsthand what it felt like to be betrayed, I would never do that to someone else. EVER.

Although this was my rule, thanks to Jessie's lie, I had done just that.

I splashed some water on my face, rinsed my mouth as best I could without a toothbrush in sight, and opened the door. I really needed a toothbrush. I felt dirty.

4

BLACK OUT RAGE!

I would like to say that I got clarification from Jessie and that all my questions were answered. I didn't.

When I left the bathroom, I packed my stuff back in my bag, got dressed, and stood by the door. I waited as he gathered his things, and we headed out for the truck. The ride back was silent at first, but he eventually turned the radio on.

> *Whore Tip: When you betray someone in your life, there is nothing that can excuse it. If you are not happy, then move on. You are hurting the other person even if they don't know it.*

I stared out the window with a million things racing through my head. The time we had spent together was amazing and with one sentence it was ruined. "I'm married." It hurt me more than I wanted something like this to. The whole point of having playmates was not to let emotions come into the arrangement. By the time he pulled into my driveway, I was hungry and angry, and I felt disgusting. Before he could say anything, I basically jumped out of the car and headed in the house.

I don't know if he attempted to follow me. I didn't care.

Throwing my bag down, I headed to the shower. I took off everything and let the hot water cover me until it ran cold. Wrapping my hair and body in a towel, I brushed my teeth for several more minutes than I am sure they needed and finally looked into the mirror. It was still fogged from the shower. This was good. I wasn't sure if I could deal with all the emotions that were flooding back now.

I decided calling Alex would be too brutal right now. She was too blunt for what I could take.

I debated calling Lucy, but she had just broken up with her boyfriend of four months. This didn't seem like a long time to most people, but to Lucy, this was difficult. Talking to her a few nights ago involved a lot of crying and reassurances that there was in fact a man out in the world who would find her clingy behavior cute.

> *Whore Tip: Never assume that what one person finds terribly annoying or weird is not something another person will find adorable. Work on the parts of you that you believe need to be fixed, not what others say.*

A call to Sally was out of the question. Where Alex would be too blunt, Sally would be overly consoling. I needed a balance.

Grabbing the phone, I was going to dial Baley. She would know how to make me not feel as horrible as I did right now. She would listen and tell me it wasn't my fault, all the things I wanted to hear. I didn't want to face that I was having more emotions than I should about what had happened.

Jessie wasn't my boyfriend. He was a playmate, a long-standing playmate, but that was all he was supposed to be. I knew that the core of my anger was because my last actual relationship ended because I had been cheated on. There was not a great playbook for getting over that happening, and I had just done it to someone else... again.

Finding out a playmate or potential playmate had an "other half" happened more than once. I hoped that after a year, I had become better at detecting this. Apparently, I had not.

Before I could hit the dial button, I got a text. If it was Jessie, I might be buying a new phone later from throwing it across the room. Then I remembered I had blocked his number.

> *Whore Tip: Never delete a number. Always block it or label it something like "Loser Club – Brad." That way years or months from now you don't get a random text or call and find out that you don't want to respond.*

The text said: *Hey Gorgeous, you busy?*
It was Marc. Now, that could be a great distraction.

5

TATTOOED BUDDHA

The text from Marc was exactly what I needed to pop me out of the spiral I was heading down. I replied: *Not yet. But if you are up for playing... I could be.* I included a kiss emoji that I hoped came across as flirty and not over eager.

> *Whore Tip: Even if you want something super badly, take a breath. Desperation is like body odor; it makes it easy for people to run away.*

He replied almost instantly: *My place or yours?*
Yours. I really needed to stop staring at my walls.
Get here soon!!!
I replied with a wink.
That was easy. But then again, it was supposed to be.

> *Whore Tip: Any Friends with Benefits arrangement should be stress relieving. Honestly, if you find yourself stressing about any aspect of it, you should take a good hard look at whether it is giving you what you need.*

Drying myself off quickly, I picked a cute bra and panties. They didn't match, in case you were wondering. In some cases, matching undergarments could get you a little something extra in the encounter. In this case, I knew it wouldn't.

I pulled on jeans and cute top, slid on my flip flops, and took a look in the mirror. My hair was messy and still a little wet, but short of wasting time using a blow dryer and straightener, it would have to stay that way. Also, Marc liked his women as natural as possible. This made it amazingly easy to go see him.

Adding a little mascara and eyebrow pencil to just slightly enhance my hazel eyes, I was super happy that I didn't let my rage turn into grief. Puffy eyes were not as easy to get rid of.

Grabbing a hoodie and my keys, I headed to Marc's.

He lived about forty minutes from me. I met him online on one of those sites you use mainly for hooking up. That is not saying that you can't meet your next "other half" on one of those, but they are very convenient for meeting a Mr. or Ms. Right Now. Also, shopping by swipe is simply a new level of laziness for women.

Marc had olive skin, dark hair, and brown eyes. He was slightly taller than me at 6'2" with a sexy square jaw. He was attractive, but I would never refer to him as cute. One of his best features as far as I was concerned was his tattoos. He was covered in ink. They decorated his arms, legs, and chest, including a large Buddha on this back. They were one of the main reasons I swiped on his profile.

I knocked on the door, and he let me in to the small apartment which suited him perfectly. With minimal furniture, the room was lit by candles, and I could smell incense burning. The best part was that he wore only a sarong.

As he closed the door, he came up behind me and began kissing my neck awhile wrapping his arms around my waist. "You smell yummy," he growled.

I moved my hands behind my back and undid the knot holding the sarong in place. He growled again as he bit at my neck a little more before grabbing my top and pulling it over my head in one quick motion.

He undid my bra and let it fall forward, sliding the straps down my arms.

"I have been thinking about you." His voice was barely a whisper in my ear.

"Oh really?"

"I have been thinking about having your juices all over my lips," he said, his tongue licking up the edge of my ear.

"Oh really...?" My voice was a breathy moan.

"I... Just... Want... To... Feel... How...Wet...You...Get...For...Me!" Each word was said with a kiss down my back and around my waist until he stood in front of me.

He placed his hands on either side of my face and pulled my lips to his. I closed my eyes and opened up to him. My tongue chased his. He was so hungry for me, and I let myself get lost in the sensation of him.

His hands explored my arms and then up from my hips to my breasts. My nipples were hard, and when his fingertips grabbed hold and tugged, I bit down on his lips a little.

I felt his hands move down and tug at the button, then the zipper of my jeans. Without breaking our contact, he moved me around, guiding me toward where I knew his couch was.

He stopped right as the back of my legs touched the couch, and he kissed down my neck and then to my chest. His hands still roaming, he took each breast into his hands. He held them up to his mouth, so he could suck each nipple separately, and then he pushed them both together, sucking hard enough to cause a little pain but knowing exactly when to stop.

He then kissed down my stomach, lowering himself to his knees. As he did, I spread my legs so they were a small distance apart. I looked down at his smiling face. Running my hands through his hair, I tugged a little to pull his head back. He ran his hands up my jeans to where he had opened them, and he grabbed hold of the top on each side, taking my panties in his hands as well and began to pull them down. He moved his mouth to where the fabric had been.

Feeling his warm breath against my skin, I ran my fingertips though his hair. I was doing this to steady myself as he had pulled everything down past my hips, but he had only begun to expose the top of my lips. He used the tip of his tongue to force his way between the top of my folds.

I moaned this time, louder and tugging on the hair in my hands.

He lowered the pants more, now exposing all of my pussy to him. He pushed his mouth into me, licking and moving his tongue. He found my center and pushed his tongue against it, sending shivers through my entire body. My legs began to shake.

He pulled his face back and looked up, my wetness glistening on his lips. "I love how wet you get," he said, pulling my pants the rest of the way down. He only looked away long enough to help guide my feet out of them.

After I had all clothes removed, he pushed me back to sit on the couch. He was still on his knees, and he pulled me toward him, so my cheeks were right on the edge. Then he spread my legs apart and lifted them, placing one on each shoulder. His mouth was on my wetness again.

My moans were almost a scream. He licked and sucked, brining me to climax within moments. It was so intense, and before I could recover, his mouth was on me again. My hands pulled at the cushions around me, grabbing the back of the couch to hold on from the sensations shooting though my body. He sucked at just the right spot, and it sent me again into orgasmic bliss.

My legs trembled uncontrollably as he lowered them to the floor, kneeling again in front of me. I could see he was perfectly erect. He held his cock in his hand, stroking himself, his face still glistening with my wetness. He eyes met mine and he smiled, his grip tightening as his hand moved. He moved in closer to me so that as his hand moved up and down his length, his knuckles grazed my lips, sending all new tremors throughout my body. I grabbed my breasts, rubbing and tugging at my own nipples, adding to the sensations.

I couldn't take my eyes off of him. His gaze was pure lust and seeing my juices all over his mouth as he grew harder with each stroke sent me over the edge again. Just as my tremors began again, he exploded onto me.

As I lay back recovering, he leaned over, grabbed the sarong, and wiped his cum off of both of us and then my cum off his face. After, he got up and went into the kitchen.

When I could stand, I went into the bathroom to get myself cleaned up.

> *Whore Tip: Make sure you take care of all your parts.*
> *Cleaning up is just as important as getting dirty.*

When I came out of the bathroom, all cleaned up, Marc handed me a glass of cool water.

"How are you doing?" he asked.

I took a sip of the water before I smiled and said, "Better now." He smiled back and didn't press further. We chatted for a little while about his weekend. He had gone to one of those concerts that featuring several bands no one had heard of. I let him tell me all about it and even play me a couple songs.

His enthusiasm was nice, but I found myself falling back into thoughts of what my weekend had been like. I got dressed and told him that I had to be up early for work. I am not sure if he believed me, but if he had any doubts, he didn't show them.

He kissed me deeply as I was walking out the door. I took one last look at him smiling at me. Maybe he was a little cute.

6

Still Visiting
Funky-Town

When I got in the car, I noticed that my phone was not there. For a moment, I thought I might have left it upstairs with Marc. However, replaying the fun we had, I knew that I had only taken my keys upstairs with me because they fell loudly out of my pocket when the jeans came off.

I searched around and remembered that I had left it on the counter in the bathroom. I think part of me didn't want it nearby because Jessie had still been trying to contact me. Shit! I didn't want to think about him. So, I did the only thing that I could think of: cranked the music up and sang my heart out all the way home.

> *Whore Tip: Always sing like no one is watching...*
> *especially when you are at karaoke!*

When I arrived home, I went into the bathroom to find my phone had died. I took it into the bedroom to charge it. I plugged it in and stripped down, getting into some comfy pjs. Just as I let out a huge breath, you know the kind you don't even know that you are holding, the phone started dinging and vibrating wildly to the point it fell off the nightstand.

Apparently, I had missed *several* texts from Sally:

Hi!

Hello?

Are you alive? 😊

You haven't checked in...???

OMG! Answer me!

Are you ignoring me?

Don't ignore me!!!

You're scaring me...please text me in the next 5 mins.

SERIOUSLY RANDI!

Fine! I am going to call Jessie now!

... called Jessie.

When you're ready to talk, let me know. 😞

Love you!

It is important to have a safety net. Sally was that for me—the nicest one of my friends. Also, the fact that she was now married to one of my childhood friends was a huge bonus. They were the perfect nerdy couple.

Whore Tip: If you are going to have playmates, you make sure that someone, even a note on your fridge, knows where you are, who you are with, and any details you have. Remember that you don't actually know this person you are meeting.

I texted back:

Call you in a few... phone charging.

I got back a *K* then followed by an *OK... Sorry...*

For the record I feel that simply sending a "K" is the text equivalent of "Fuck-Off" in text lingo. It takes moments to send a text in response and nothing timewise to add an additional letter. I have told my friends this, and I make a point the first time a new playmate sends one of the offending Ks to explain all of the feelings I have on this point. I have stopped talking to men because of it. You might be thinking this is stupid. It isn't. I assure you.

Whore Tip: Hold true to those things that you believe. You don't have to be stubborn; just don't find yourself bending to the point of breaking. You can choose.

Making myself a drink and grabbing some chips, I moved the charging phone to the living-room and dialed Sally, putting her on speaker.

"Heya! Are you okay?" That's how she answered the phone.

"Yeah. I am still pissed, but I went and saw Buddha," I said, stuffing some chips into my mouth.

"Wait!" She was surprised. "You got home and then went right out for a rendezvous?"

I was still chewing. "Yep"

"Seriously?" Alright, maybe it was shock and not surprise.

I took a sip of my drink. "What? What is wrong with having a distraction right now?"

Sally sighed. "Will you tell me what happened?"

"With Jessie or Buddha?" I asked, already knowing the answer. "What did Jessie say when you talked to him?" I didn't like the feeling as I let those words escape my lips. I found myself wanting to hear how he wanted me. How he missed me. It made me feel uncomfortable. This wasn't good for me.

"Well, it was weird," she started. "When he answered, I had to explain who I was and why I was calling."

"What did you say?" I asked, stifling a laugh. The thought of Sally trying to engage in a conversation with a playmate with the sole intention of trying to find out if they had caused me to be listed as a "missing person" was hysterical.

"The whole thing doesn't matter. He just ended up saying that he was sorry and that you were not speaking to him anymore." She took a breath. "Did you break up or something?" Her question was innocent enough. My laughter disappeared. "No," I said simply. "He's married."

Sally started offering all kinds of support, but I found myself unable to hear any of it. I had been having playdates with Jessie for just over a year and the fact was it did feel a bit like a break up. Like I had been cheated on all over again. Though, this time, I was the one at the center of the cheating.

Eventually, I told Sally I had to go. I did not want to talk about it anymore. Knowing that I had been cheating with Jessie on his wife for over a year was devastating. Any residual thoughts of Marc faded, and I ended the night by eating a pint of ice cream and sending all of Jessie's emails directly into the trash.

Whore Tip: It is important to be willing to experience the bad things in life. Just remember: it is okay to make mistakes. Just try to

ensure they are new ones and not repeats.

7

Bartender Grab Bag

On Friday night around eleven, my phone started ringing. I looked down to see it was Baley. I had been avoiding men for a couple months—which also meant I had not been going out much. I really needed to get myself back to the place where I was comfortable with just one- night stands. Or maybe a couple night stands. What happened with Jessie proved that there was a point when emotions started to form, and I should have stopped it when that happened.

> *Whore Tip: Make sure you know where your feelings are in any relationship. Having certainty of this will allow you to make the right decisions.*

"Hello?"

"Get ready. No more moping. We are going out!" Baley was way too excited.

"I dunno...."

I couldn't finish before she said, "You have an hour. Be ready!" and hung up.

Looking at the phone, I started to text her, then stopped. Continuing to lock myself in the house would only prove that I was not in control. I was. Dating was like riding a bike after all.

Baley arrived exactly at midnight. She was like my fairy god-mother in a cute shirt and super-tight jeans. Her red hair was up in a messy bun, and she had perfect smoky eyes. Gesturing behind her, she said, "Let's go. Lucy is waiting for us." With that, we jumped in the Uber she had ordered.

I asked her where we were headed, and she told me that a local bar called Chic-a-Boom was holding a mid-year-new-years. In case you are wondering what that means, they were giving away free champagne to the ladies that night. It is always interesting the lengths bars and clubs will go to in order to have as many ladies arrive as possible.

When we walked in, Lucy was already at the log bar in the front. She waved us over, and as we walked up, she handed us each a Green Tea shot. We held up the glasses, and Lucy scrunched her eyes for a moment, smiled, and said, "To remembering the good things!" We clinked our shot glasses together and downed them in one gulp. She was quick to hand me another and leaned in with a wink, "Just in case." I smiled back at her and downed that one too.

> *Whore Tip: If you have never had one, you should*
> *try a Green Tea shot. It consists of Jameson Whiskey,*
> *Peach Schnapps, Sour Mix, and Lemon-Lime Soda.*
> *It is always a good idea to find new favorites.*

Lucy told us that they were giving out the champagne at the bar in the back, which meant we would need to travel through the dance floor between the two bars. "Let's go shake our asses a bit then!" Lucy said and began moving in the direction of the loud music.

We made our way to the dance floor and saw there was a band that night. The lead singer announced that this was going to be their last song just as we found a spot after weaving into the crowd. The bar was on a tourist route in Florida, after all. The crowd was a mix of locals and out of towners and would make for a good hunting ground—if one were so inclined.

The band started to play, and it turned out that they had a surprisingly good rock sound. I scanned around to see if there were any prospects. Are you wondering if I was ready to go because I had a couple of shots in me? The answer was No. This was more out of habit than anything. It actually takes a bit of skill to scan the room. If you are not careful, you make eye contact with the wrong person and awkwardness abounds.

As I continued the scan around the room, I spotted a friend of mine at the bar. I told Baley that I was going to go over and say hi. She nodded, looking over to where I was pointing. Making my way through the crowd, I arrived at a small high-top table and tapped the shoulder of my friend Archer. He was chatting with an extremely cute guy wearing a black V-neck and a girl who looked like she dressed like a fifties pin-up girl. Archer turned to see me and immediately smiled. Giving me a hug and kiss on the cheek, he introduced me to his friends Amy and Zach.

"What are you doing here? Or should I ask: *Who* are you doing here?" His voice was playful.

"I'm here with Baley and Lucy." I pointed over to where they had been standing when I left them. "Free champagne lures the females."

Archer was the same height as me at six feet, and he was slender with an angular face. He owned a high-end salon and was one of the main reasons I looked the way I did. Because he was my hairdresser, he had been privy to many of the stories of my exploits.

"So, are you on the hunt tonight or did you pre-arrange your meal?" He smiled at his own wit.

"Not sure. I think I will see where the night takes me," I replied.

"I, for one, cannot wait to hear where the night takes you," he said as he tilted his glass and then downed the rest of the contents.

We chatted for a couple of minutes as he told me that they were headed out to a late-night Tapas restaurant for some artisanal cocktails and food. I hugged him again and told Amy and Zach it was nice to meet them, making a mental note that I must ask Archer about Zach when I was next in his chair. From my brief interaction, he was very nice to look at.

I scanned to see if Lucy and Baley were where I had left them, but the normal club music had started, and the band was breaking down their equipment. I decided to check in the general direction of the free champagne.

The bar area in the back was a large open area with several high-top tables and two pool tables. It had some cover, but half of it was open to the wonderful and sometimes very humid Florida air. Since it was wintertime, the weather was actually a little chilly but nice. One of the best reasons for living in central Florida was that it never snowed.

I saw that Lucy and Baley were at the bar, and Baley now wore a white fedora hat. They gestured me over. There was a man leaning in to speak with them, and as I approached, Lucy did the Big Eyes.

Whore Tip: Always have a gesture you can do with your friends so that you can signal when you are in trouble. In our case, it is opening our eyes super wide as if it is the most surprising moment of our life: aka the Big-Eyes.

As I got to the bar, the man turned. He was older, possibly late fifties, with white hair and wearing a linen button-down shirt.

"Is this her?" he asked, slurring his words.

"Yep," Baley said. "That's her."

The man grabbed my hand and kissed it before I could pull it away. "Congratulations, Beautiful," he said, slurring so the words he actually said were: "Con-tag-your-lat-shuns Boo-tiff-ull."

I looked over to Lucy, who offered, "This is Albert. He is apparently not-Jewish, and B here told him about your engagement and how that is why we're here tonight."

Confusion played across my features for a moment. "Not Jewish?" I asked. Baley nodded. "I see." I watched him sway a little. "Is that his hat?" Baley nodded again, smirking.

"So," he said moving in closer to me, "are you in an open relationship?"

Wow. This was going to be fun.

I looked around quickly and noticed a guy with curly brown hair with a nice-trimmed beard. I grabbed his hand, saying, "There you are, Honey!" Since I was facing away from Albert, I attempted Big Eyes and hoped he caught on.

"Ummm...." he said, but he didn't pull his hand back from mine—a good sign.

"Honey," I said, leaning into him, "this is Albert," I gestured with my open hand, "and he wants to congratulate us on our engagement."

"You are a lucky dog!" Albert said, reaching out his hand. I was silently hoping this would work.

"John," my new friend said, grasping Albert's hand and shaking it. "I agree I am very lucky," he continued, leaning in to kiss me firmly on the lips.

He was a good kisser, and as he pulled back, I smiled, biting a little on my lower lip.

I heard someone clear their throat. Albert was still staring at us, waiting. "I am sorry, Albert. John and I are *NOT* in an open relationship."

It was John's turn to look confused. However, he recovered quickly and put his arm around me, pulling me closer to him. "I couldn't share my goddess with anyone." He was almost too good at this.

Albert looked back and forth between us again. Then turned back to the girls and asked them, "Which one do I get to take home tonight, or can I have both?"

A look of true disgust crossed Lucy's face, and my new fiancé looked behind him and got the attention of a bouncer gesturing him over.

When the bouncer arrived, John whispered something to him, and the bouncer helped Albert find the exit, which included Baley giving up the hat as Albert congratulated me and John again on his way out.

"Thank you," I said to John when Albert was out of earshot.

"You're welcome...umm...?"

"Randi," I said with a smile, "and this is Baley and Lucy." He shook their hands. "So, are we having a big wedding?" He was smirking now.

"No. I think it should be a small intimate affair. Family and close friends only." He had a very sexy smile.

"We should celebrate. It is not every day I meet my future wife." With that, he walked past us and around the bar. Watching him, I thought he was either spontaneous or crazy as he uncorked a bottle and put it along with three glasses in front of us.

"For my lovely bride," he said with that sexy smile again. "This bottle is on the house."

"Hmmm... and I thought the champagne was free tonight?" Lucy said playfully.

"It is...But I expect a big tip for my services," he said with a wink.

> *Whore Tip: Always be willing to have fun and allow yourself to go out of your comfort zone. You never know where it might take you.*

"Speaking of services," I turned to the girls as he poured the drinks, "do I want to ask why the hell that just happened?" Lucy and Baley looked at each other and just shook their head no in unison.

John laughed.

It turned out that John was the head bartender of Chic-a-boom. He was twenty-eight and spent the next couple of hours flirting with me, pouring us glasses of champagne in between customers until we had finished off three bottles and moved into our fourth.

As he set the bottle on the bar, he crooked his finger in a come closer gesture toward me. I leaned in to meet him halfway across the bar, and he whispered in my ear, "Want to help me count some boxes of champagne in the stock room?" I looked over toward the girls who both nodded, and I replied, "I'm very good at counting."

He smiled, moved back out of the bar area, and led me to a door that was cleverly hidden in the hallway near the bathroom. We slipped inside the stock room with him leading. It was exactly what I expected. There were boxes and bottles on shelves and piled along the walls. He led me around a set of shelves, so we were out of view from anyone who walked in the door.

I was a little drunk, which probably made this much more feasible because any voice that would tell me to stop because it was still too soon was passed out in the corner of my brain.

Not waiting a moment more, I grabbed his face and brought it to mine, kissing him deeply. Our tongues played with each other as his hands wrapped around me, pulling me closer before sliding down to my ass and grabbing it firmly. A moan escaped my lips.

He pulled back for a moment, almost growling, "God, you're so fucking hot." With this, I pushed my lips against his again, running my fingers through his hair, pulling him closer to me. His hands moved to slide under my shirt and over my bra, tugging on my now hard nipples. I moaned again and tilted my head back. He kissed my neck then with little bites, and his hands moved down to undo the button on the top of my jeans and unzip them.

His hand moved into my jeans, and sliding my panties aside, he found my wet folds. The first touch sent shivers through me, and I moaned louder, grabbing hold of his pants and undoing the button and zipper as well.

He used the tip of his index finger to gently rub my nub. I moved my hips with his motions. I slid my hand in his pants to find that he was hard. Because he was pointed downward, I gently moved his hard cock so it pointed upward. As I did this, he held his breath for just a moment, stopping the motion on my now very wet pussy.

> *Whore Tip: Pay attention to your partner's body language to know when you are in a danger zone or have passed their line in the sand. You never want them to go where they are not comfortable. The same rule applies for you as well.*

"Don't worry," I purred. "I won't break it; I want to be able to play."

This was all he needed to slide his fingers inside me. I held on to his shoulder with one hand and his hard member with the other.

I stroked him up and down and found that he was a great length and girth. I found myself imagining that cock sliding inside of me as he pushed in another finger. My strokes got faster as I began to explode.

My grip tightened on his shoulder as he moved his thumb, rubbing my clit, and I came hard. I felt my walls spasm around his fingers as the noises I was making drove him over the edge and he exploded.

Taking care, as did he, I removed my hand from his pants as we heard the door swing open. He pulled his hand out of mine when a female voice said, "John, you in here?" He moved past me so he could look around the corner. "Yeah, what's up?"

"Travis is looking for you. He is not happy," his coworker told him.

"Be right there," John replied quickly.

I finished buttoning my jeans as he turned around. I wasn't sure how my make-up fared, but I wasn't too worried.

"Unscheduled break? Hope you're not in trouble," I teased as he grabbed a bar towel off the shelf and turned to clean himself up.

"How can I get into trouble spending time with my wife to be?" he said, smirking as he looked back over his shoulder.

"True" was all I said, smiling back.

He peeked out the door to make sure it was clear. I slipped out to go to the ladies' room, and he left, I assumed in search of Travis.

The girls were ready to head out when I got back to the bar, and Baley called for another Uber. John had not returned to the bar by the time we made our way out to the street to meet our ride. When it pulled up and the girls got in, I felt a tap on my shoulder. It was John. He grabbed my hand, slid a ring made of paper onto my finger, and planted one last kiss on my lips before running back inside.

The girls wanted all the details on the way home, which unfortunately or fortunately for our driver, I shared without leaving anything out. Baley was still pissed she had lost the white fedora, and I told her we would search for one as soon as possible.

When I got home, I slid the paper ring off my finger and opened it. It was, of course, his number. I put it in my phone as John – Bar Fiancé.

The whole night proved only one thing: I was back.

THE BLAKE SITUATION

W e have now arrived at the person Alex and I were discussing at coffee earlier.

I met Blake online, swiping right on Tinder.

Tinder, like so many apps, is the Instacart of "dating" online. You can grab it anytime, put some items in your cart, then decide if you want to buy. If you don't want to buy something, you can always put it back: aka unlike.

> *Whore Tip: Remember when hunting, one of the partners has an advantage. Also, make sure you are speaking the same language. You will not change what the other person is looking for.*

Blake had just moved down from up north. He worked for a power company designing grid traffic. I found this out only after meeting him. I asked him why he would move to a state like Florida, full of hurricanes which inevitably led to power issues. He said it offered more excitement.

I was honest with my intentions. When we ended up talking, he had a lot of questions for me. Like many of my playmates, he did not believe me when I first explained that I was not looking for strings to be attached.

He wanted to know if I was seeing anyone else right then. I thought about the bartender, but I had not decided if I should text him yet. I answered honestly, "No."

Looking back, I let the conversation go on longer than I should have. It seemed like we had a lot in common actually, and Blake asked me if he could take me out to dinner. I agreed.

His company had put him up in a hotel while he found an apartment. Having been here only three days, he was still on the hunt. Apparently hunting for female companionship was more important than a place to live since he told me he hadn't seen any apartments yet. Priorities are important.

I knew what going out to dinner meant. It takes longer than a drink, and unless you are horribly rude, you do not generally have an easy out. I found that Blake was fun to talk to and when I explained it might be worth trying to go on a date... well Alex, as you know, reacted very badly.

She had a point. Several actually.

> *Whore Tip: If you have friends whose advice you trust, it is worth it to take a moment or two listening to them. Sometimes you cannot see an issue because you are too deep in the muck.*

Needless to say, I decided to take the plunge anyway and see if I could steer this back to what I called a "Dine-and-Dash."

Leaving all the details with Sally, I headed to a Mexican restaurant called Carmelita's near his hotel. He told me he would meet me outside so we could head in together.

On Tinder, he had a baseball cap in almost every photo. He had strawberry blonde hair, the parts you could see, blue eyes, and a cute smile. His pictures showed that he was a little overweight, so when I got to the restaurant, I was slightly surprised that he was more than just a little overweight. He was very chubby. He was wearing a button-down shirt, cargo shorts, and sneakers.

As I walked up, he smiled. He was cute.

"Hi Blake," I said.

"Well, hello Randi," he said, still smiling. He was nervous.

We had an awkward handshake or hug moment, and he ended up holding the door so we could head inside.

When we sat down, he didn't remove his cap, which was a little surprising.

I knew we were here to casually meet up, but this seemed a little more casual which helped me push this back into the playmate category.

The waitress came up to the table, dropping off chips, and asked for our drink order. I decided to go margarita on the rocks, since they were two for one, and Blake ordered a beer.

"So... Randi, where do you work?" he asked, over the menu he held.

"Oh, I work... in an office," I replied, a little puzzled, still trying to decide if tacos were too messy for this type of meeting. Alex's voice spoke in my head again: *This is a bad idea.*

"I know that. What do you do?" His tone was curious and trying to be playful.

"What are you going to get?" I tried to change the topic. "I am thinking either tacos or enchiladas."

Like a magic trick, it worked. Not surprisingly, Blake was a foodie. He went into an entire explanation of the various Mexican food he liked to prepare. He finished his story by telling me about how he could not wait to set up his kitchen and have me over for dinner.

Putting a future there. Yikes!!

Whore Tip: Lies always, always, always will bite you
in the butt at some point and never in a good way.

At that moment, the waitress brought over our drinks. Conveniently for me, she brought both of my margaritas, and I was able to not-so-casually down the first one quickly.

"So, what are some of your favorite meals to prepare?" I asked Blake after setting my glass on the edge of the table.

Again, the magic worked, and I listened to him explain all kinds of things about his skills in the kitchen. It wasn't boring or close to torture. It was making the night go by with less probing questions on my real life that I was not sure I wanted to share.

Alex was right. I knew it. I was not ready to date.

When the meal arrived, I ordered my second round of drinks. I had chosen to go with the tacos because I was afraid he would want to try some of my enchiladas if I ordered it. Sharing food or drinks was something you should only do with close friends or people you are dating.

When the waitress asked if we wanted dessert, I was full, but Blake ordered something to go. He insisted on paying for dinner, and when we got up to leave, he asked me if I wanted to come up and hang out for a bit.

It might have been the tequila talking, but I said yes and followed him to his hotel.

9

PRESTON MONTAGUE
BRAXTON THE THIRD

When we got back to the hotel, I would like to say that passions were burning and we pulled each other's clothes off. Actually, when we arrived at his room, and he slid the key card in the lock to open the door, I heard snuffling and barking. He entered the room first, and as I followed him in, he was petting a small black pug that was now jumping up and down.

It should be noted at this time that I love animals. I do. With this love of our furry, feathered, and scaly friends, I have also concluded that I am not a dog person. It actually isn't dogs specifically. It is more any animals that need constant attention. This is why I love cats. Because most cats decide when they will grant you their attention and not the other way around. As I am stating this, I realize that it might in fact reflect my life right now.

He picked up the pug and turned around. "Randi, this is Preston," and pet the dog's ear with his finger.

Preston had his tongue hanging out, super happy to be in the company of humans. Most dogs were like this.

Whore Tip: When it comes to animals and being with someone, be honest with yourself first before telling the

person you are fine with them. It is more likely you
will have to like their pets even more than their family.

I reached out to give Preston a little pet, and he licked my hand before I could even touch him. "Aww... Preston Montague Braxton the Third likes you," Blake said in a tone you use for pets and small children. My face wasn't hiding anything. I heard Alex laugh little.

"Wow, your dog sounds like a prep-school trust fund kid," I tried in vain to make a little joke as I turned back toward the bathroom. "I am just going to wash my hands." When I returned from the bathroom, Blake was sitting in the middle of the bed. He had turned down the lights so there was just a bedside lamp.

He smiled and patted the bed for me to join him. I looked around and the dog was sitting in its bed with a treat.

Note to past self: This is the point I should have walked out of the room.

Instead, I slipped off my shoes and sat on the bed next to him

He leaned in and began kissing me. Surprisingly, he was a good kisser. His lips were soft at first, but then he slid his hand around the back of my neck, grabbing my hair, and he pushed his tongue between my lips.

I closed my eyes and let his hands begin to move down my arm and over to my breasts. For a moment as his fingertips encircled my nipples, I thought that I could have this experience.

Then I heard it. Whimpering. Soft at first.

I broke from the kiss and looked down. Preston was pacing around the end of the bed.

Blake tugged at my nipple and kissed my neck.

I closed my eyes again and slid my hand up Blake's leg to his now hard cock.

Whimper

Blake slid his hands down my leg.

Whimper

Whimper

Bark

I pulled back and looked at Blake, then down at the dog who was now circling around the bed and whimpering, growling, and barking.

"No Preston! No! Go lay down!" Blake took the tone again with more sternness.

Whimper

The dog continued to circle.

Whine

Whine

Bark

Blake leaned back to resume activities.

Whine

"Seriously?" I asked, gesturing down at the dog now in almost a tizzy.

Whine

Whimper

"Just ignore him," he said, smiling and trying for a pouty face.

Bark

Whimper

"I'm sorry... But..." I wasn't able to finish as he placed his finger on my lips.

Whine

Bark

BARK–BARK–BARK

I stood up from the bed. Preston started jumping on my leg and running under my feet, and I almost tripped on him. Blake stood up as well and tried to come up behind me and wrap his arms around me.

BARK – GROWL – BARK – WHIMPER – WHINE – BARK

I turned to him, "Goodnight," and then turned back and headed for the door. I would like to say my leaving was just as smooth as it sounded, but I had to wait until Blake grabbed Preston to actually make my exit. Blake was trying to make all kinds of excuses and reasons I should not go. I tuned them out.

Is it terrible that the thought of just opening the door and walking out floated through my thoughts for longer than a moment? Alas, it was not Preston's fault.

I pinged the Uber on the way down to the lobby and walked outside to wait. I was lucky it only took a couple minutes for them to arrive. As we drove, I could smell the dog on my clothes, Blake obviously let him sleep in the bed. Now his actions made sense. Preston suffered from a little green monster.

I called Alex the next day and told her the whole story. I am not sure she heard it through all the laughter.

Blake texted me several times over the next few weeks. I thought of responding, but he didn't check a single box on my playmate list, and he would never have been a dating prospect. What can I say? I am not a dog person.

> *Whore Tip: As horrible as it sounds, sometimes you have the slam the door shut and keep it closed. If you answer, even to say you're not interested, you are basically saying, "There is a chance."*

10

THE PIT STOP

R oad trips are one of my favorite experiences, especially when it is with friends. Exploring new places. Finding fun local food. Meeting local people and getting invited to local hangouts when they flirt back with you.

I was lucky enough that Archer asked me to accompany him on a trip to Boston to see his girlfriend. We left on Thursday morning pretty early with coffee in hand.

When I asked if his friend Zach would be joining us, he warned me that I really didn't want to go there. When I asked why I didn't, he simply said to trust him and would not elaborate more.

We decided we would make one stop on the way up whenever we got hungry for dinner. This made it more of an adventure.

It was around 9pm when we finally decided the need to "feed the beast" as Archer put it was required. We pulled off the highway at a small town somewhere between North Carolina or Virginia. There was a sign for a BBQ restaurant called Boss Hogs, which is a play on the Dukes of Hazzard. I would love to run into Bo or Luke Duke while I was here.

When we got inside, it was the kind of place where there were hubcaps on the wall, peanuts on the floor, and the waitresses looked like they had been working there for years. They seemed to know all the regulars by name.

We were sat at a table, and when asked what beer they had on tap, it was every kind of Bud product you can imagine. We were lucky that they had some bottles of Corona, but no lime. We ordered a bucket, which is six if you are keeping track. For dinner, we ordered a rack of ribs, some chicken, sides, and garlic bread.

The thing about BBQ is there is not a delicate way to eat it. You are bound to get sauce all over your hands and face.

> *Whore Tip: Remember when going out to eat with a potential playmate or date to choose your food wisely. You do not want to show your caveman side until you have racked up plenty of plus points.*

When the beer arrived, I think we both downed the first one in minutes. The food was amazing, and we got stuffed way before we ran out of things to eat. When the waitress offered dessert, we both simply groaned and shook our heads no.

We asked her where the best place to stay in town was, and she told us of a cute family-run motel up the road. "Clean sheets and good people." In a small town, this was a good compliment. There was a bar called Red's right across the street, and she said we wouldn't be able to miss it. With that, we headed out.

The motel was easy to check into, and the rooms were super clean and cute. They even had the little plastic diamond-shaped room keys and rotary phones in the room. This also meant that we would have to actually check out in the morning at the front desk. So quaint!

Archer and I decided to take a shower to wash off the road and the BBQ, and then head over for a couple more drinks before bed.

Walking across the street, we saw quickly that Red's was a biker bar. It had a dirt parking lot and music floating out the door. As we approached, the bouncer sized us up. I think it was more the skinny jeans that Archer was wearing because it definitely screamed that we were not from around there. He didn't check our IDs, waving us right inside.

We walked in and there was a bar to the right in an L shape. Two pool tables sat to the left along with several little four-seater tables and a stage in the corner.

A curvy waitress walked past us, her red hair reminding myself of me if I was working in a dive bar in a town along a highway. She smiled at Archer, who abruptly turned and headed to the bar.

"Wonder if that is the Red the bar is named after?" I said, and he looked back her way as she shimmied between tables.

"I would name a bar after her," he replied.

We turned back to the bar and ordered a couple of beers, sticking with our alcohol choice for the evening. The music started up again with a very tall muscular man on the stage. He had a microphone in his hand and began to sing "Mustang Sally" in a deep voice.

"Now, that is what I would name a bar after," I said, gesturing to him with my beer mug. Archer smiled. "Always hunting."

I pushed on his shoulder a bit teasingly, then continued to watch the show.

There was something oddly familiar about the man on stage. He wore jeans, the straight-legged kind, a pair of work boots, and t-shirt that clung to every muscle. I took another sip of my beer, gesturing again at the man singing. "Who does he remind you of?"

"What do you mean?"

"I mean, who does he look like? The singer?"

"Your next meal?" He chuckled at his own joke.

"Seriously!" I knew Archer wasn't torturing me on purpose, but it was mildly irritating not to have someone else answer the question plaguing my brain.

We continued to watch until the song was done, and we clapped as he exited the stage. "I think we should sing a song," I blurted as I spun around back toward the bar to get the bartender's attention.

"Do you?" Archer turned around as well, amused now. "And what song do you think *we* should sing? And if you say 'Summer Lovin' from *Grease*, I am walking out of here right now."

"Four shots of Jack, please," I said to the bartender, "and two more beers." He smiled at me and headed off.

"Shots, huh?"

"Yep! We are going to do shots and then get up on that stage and sing... 'Paradise by the Dashboard light.'"

Archer began to laugh "Meatloaf? Seriously?"

"Well, you said we couldn't do *Grease*, and I do not think this crowd would appreciate a Cardi B/Bruno Mars hit. So, Meatloaf it is!" I said, just as the bartender handed us our drinks.

We both downed the shots and grabbed the beers. I toasted, "To dive bars and BBQ!" and we clinked our beers together. "Let's do this!"

As we stood up, me first and Archer reluctantly following, I scanned the bar for the big guy. He walked out of the restroom area and was heading for the bar. We made eye contact, and I winked.

> *Whore Tip: Never pass up an opportunity to flirt or do something that scares you a little. Life is about living it.*

We got to the stage, put our song in, and waited our turn. We were able to finish our beer before we were called up.

As the song started, I was quite happy the two shots were hitting me. I looked out into the bar and noticed tall, bald, and sexy was watching me or us, but I was hoping it was me.

We started singing, and it surprised the crowd how good Archer's voice was. I waited for my part and then jumped in. This was one of my favorite songs growing up, and I had sung it a million times in the car. I didn't need to read the monitor for the words.

When we got done, the patrons of the bar were clapping, and I had to pee.

I told Archer that I would meet him back at the bar and went to the ladies' room located right off the stage. The bathroom was exactly as you are picturing it now.

When I returned to the bar, I found Archer chatting with the guy from the stage. As I approached, it hit me: he looked exactly like Stone Cold Steve Austin.

"There you are," Archer said with a devilish smile.

"Peter, this magnificent creature is Randi," he said gesturing, "and Randi, this is Peter."

I reached out a hand that was still a little damp from the sink. I hadn't wanted to touch anything else in the bathroom. "Nice to meet you."

Peter smiled at me. "It is VERY nice to meet you." He didn't let go of my hand.

"I was just telling Peter how we were stopping just for the night. The *whole* night... you know, here. In this town." Archer was a little drunk but playing the part of the epic wingman.

"Oh yes," I smirked, "the whole night." I emphasized, giving him a suggestive look.

Peter smiled. "Wanna drink?" He hadn't taken his eyes off me.

"Yes... yes I do," I said, biting my lower lip.

"Good gravy!" he exclaimed and waved the bartender over. I ordered another shot. Peter got one for Archer as well. The thought of another beer made me think of the bathroom. That experience did not need to happen again—and definitely not before whatever was about to happen here.

After we all took the shot, Archer said he was ready to go back to the motel. I told Peter we should walk him over so that he doesn't get "lost" or anything.

Peter smiled and grabbed my hand again. "We should keep him safe," he said, and we headed back across the street.

11

GOOD GRAVY!

W hen we arrived at my motel door, I fumbled with the key. I wasn't trying to be cute; honestly, I was a little drunk and I legitimately struggled to get the key in the hole.

It did not help that he was standing behind me. Close. Remarkably close.

He placed his hands on the top of the doorframe. His scent was a combination of sweat, whiskey, and cologne. It was amazing. I felt his breath on the back of my neck. My body reacted in ways that made me want to throw the damn key on the ground and have him take me outside.

However, this thought was tempered by the fact that I could still hear the sounds from the bar across the street.

> *Whore Tip: Acts of a sexual nature in public can be naughty. Getting arrested during the act and having your mugshot online is a whole different kind of naughty. Like Santa's bad list.*

I finally got the door open, and I let him inside. I removed the key from the lock with far more ease and tossed it on the table inside.

As soon as we crossed the doorway, he spun around and picked me up. I wrapped my legs around his waist, letting him push me up against the door, closing it hard.

I wrapped my arms around his shoulders as his hands cupped my ass. His lips came dangerously close to mine, and he growled, "I want to taste you."

My tongue slid out, the tip licking around his lips. He growled again, and my panties were now soaked. He pushed himself against my core as my lips pressed into his, his tongue tangling with mine. I couldn't get enough.

I ran my fingernails over his scalp, down his neck, and pulled his face to mine. I gently bit his lower lip, pulling back to see the hunger in his blue eyes.

Spinning around quickly, he took a few steps and tossed me on the bed. He slid his boots off and then removed his shirt. Jeans were next, and then he was standing in front of me in boxer briefs, the tip of his extremely hard cock poking out the top.

I was mesmerized just looking at him from where I lay on the bed. His hand began to stroke himself on the outside of his underwear. He was teasing me. I pulled off my shoes, jeans, and top so that I was only wearing my bra and panties, then I knelt on the bed, sliding my fingers under the fabric of my panties. Two can play at his game.

For a moment, our gazes locked in a battle of wills... until I used my other hand to spring my bra loose and let it fall down my shoulder, exposing one of my ridiculously hard nipples.

His eyes widened, and he moved to me, pulling the bra the rest of the way off and throwing it across the room.

Pushing me back on the pillows so he could look down at me, he spread my knees apart and began kissing up my thighs. He made his way up, kissing, licking, and nibbling on each side. My fingers dug into the bedspread, grabbing hold as his mouth hovered above my very wet peach. The heat from his breath sent goosebumps all over me.

I felt him nuzzle the cloth until his mouth reached the band of the panties, and he used his teeth to begin pulling them off. His hands once again cupped my butt, using his fingertips to help remove the last remaining piece of clothing from my body. I was going to explode...soon.

As he pulled the panties off my legs, they closed to allow the fabric to escape. When he had flung the panties in the direction of the bra, he pushed my legs up toward my chest. Holding me at the bend of the knee with both hands, he pushed so that my bottom moved to meet his mouth.

He licked my folds up and down. Parting them with his tongue, he moved deeper, and as he touched my pleasure center, I cried out and my legs began to tremble. He added more pressure, bringing me again within moments. I dug my fingers in tighter, holding on as my body moved on its own.

So many sensations ran through me as I felt his lips encircle my throbbing nub, and he began sucking, causing me to explode again. This time he let me writhe before him.

His lips were still wet with my juices as I watched him remove the last of his clothing and throw it across the room. He looked at me expectantly.

I pointed across the room to the bags resting on the luggage rack. "The pink one," I said.

He looked a little confused but followed the directions, picking up and unzipping the small bag. It looked even smaller than normal in his hands. He looked in and recognition spread across his face.

He grabbed a condom and headed back toward me, sliding it on as he approached. I was able to see all of him, and it was nothing short of magnificent.

He was so hard that his cock bounced a little as he moved. To say he was above average was an understatement.

As he got to the edge of the bed, he held out his hand to me. I took it, and he pulled me into him. He was warm as his arms wrapped around me, and when he kissed me, I could taste myself on his lips.

"How do you want me, Peter?" I whispered into his ear.

> *Whore Tip: Most people love it when you say their name in bed. I, for one, love it. Make sure you have this tool in your arsenal.*

"I'll show you what I want, Randi," he promised in a low voice. *Could this be any more perfect?*

Lifting me up again, he slid me onto his cock, then leaned down on the bed so that his arms were still wrapped around me.

He began to thrust, using his legs to push and his arms to pull me toward him. He was so deep inside me that I could feel myself stretch to receive all of him. With each stroke, I felt him grind against my core. As I climaxed again, he pulled me up so my mouth was on his again and then he exploded.

Gently laying me on the bed, he rolled off to lay next to me. I listened to the sound of our breathing for a time.

"I am going to jump in the shower. Wanna join me?" I couldn't hide my smile.

"Get all wet with you again? Of course!" he said, kissing me.

> *Whore Tip: Sometimes you are simply lucky enough to have perfect evening. When that happens, don't let yourself ruin it.*

I met up with Archer the next morning so we could check out and head out. We still had another day's worth of driving. We stopped for breakfast right outside of town, and of course, he wanted all the details.

I think he laughed the hardest when I told him that Peter was a steel worker by trade and his full name was Peter Von Schmitt. Sometimes, you meet small town royalty. I would do this trip anytime Archer wanted company as long as we planned our stops from now on.

Good gravy!

12

I Accidentally Swallowed

After returning from the road trip by way of Red's bar again, I found myself confident on what I wanted.

I decided that if I were going to have a playmate for more than a one-time experience, I would need to allow time between them. That way I could ensure that I did not let them start filling a slot in my life they were not qualified for.

That weekend was my good friend Amber's birthday. She had set up a dinner, followed by drinks and dancing.

The restaurant she chose was a fancy brick oven pizza place. I call it fancy because the individual pizzas were over twenty dollars each, and it had an expensive wine list. The party consisted of all of us: Baley, Lucy, Alex, Sally, and me. Amber wanted it to be just the girls. She had recently started dating a previous ex, but felt he still deserved to be punished for something he had done years ago to her. Amber was tenacious and ballsy. She had tattoos of two brass knuckles on her chest. The best part was that with her big heart, she would both care for you and fight for you. The latter was very scary to witness.

After dinner, we left the restaurant, but instead of heading to a local beer bar (Alex loved craft beers), we all ended up down the road at the Chic-a-Boom bar.

The same bar John worked at.

Don't get me wrong. I enjoyed the bar and the bartender. But I had violated one of the key rules when choosing playmates.

> *Whore Tip: It is vital you do not choose playmates in establishments you may frequent again. It changes the customer/vendor relationship and not always for the better.*

I tried to explain this situation to Amber before we walked in.

"Can we go somewhere else? This night is about you."

"Of course it is about me! It is my goddamn birthday, bitches!!!" The last part may have been screamed at the top of her lungs.

"Ummm... Yeah. Can we go to the HOB?" Hoping to distract her mission, I threw out the House of Beer, the aforementioned craft beer destination. I hoped Alex would help out, but she didn't say a word.

"What is the deal?" Amber was not being dissuaded.

I looked toward Baley and Lucy who were both giggling. Sally just shrugged.

"I kinda fooled around with the bartender," I said, trying to keep my voice down.

"Which one?"

"Do you know them all?"

"Maybe. Just wondering if it is the super-hot one?"

I looked at her, confused. "And which one is the 'super-hot' one?" I asked, using air quotations.

"Did you sleep with him here?" Alex asked sarcastically.

"We didn't have sex. We only... wait. Why am I explaining this to you? Can we just not go here?" Listening to myself say this out loud, it sounded silly.

"I want shots," Amber said. "They want shots." She gestured to the rest of the girls. "Here," she said, pointing to the bar, "has shots." She huffed.

"Stop being so *tonighty,* and let's do some shots!" She headed in the door.

"Yeah, Randi... stop being so *tonighty,*" Lucy said as she, Baley, and Sally headed inside behind Amber.

"What the hell does that mean?" I looked at Alex.

"Not sure, but I think it is like being a whiny bitch." She winked and gave me a wide smile before turning and walking inside.

Whore Tip: Don't be so TONIGHTY!

When I caught up with the girls, Amber was getting shots poured for all of us. I didn't recognize the bartender. I handed over my card to cover the bill; it was her birthday after all.

After three rounds of shots, we were all absolutely ready to dance or fight. Amber had been called or texted by her new/ex/whatever boyfriend several times.

She finally put her phone in her purse after shutting it off. She ordered another round of shots. She had a story to tell us about how she and her new/ex beau were currently fighting because they had been messing around earlier, he came in her mouth, and she "accidentally swallowed." Sally spit out some of her water and the rest of us were laughing... hard.

I had to clarify.

"I'm sorry... you what?" I asked, trying to contain my mirth.

"I was sucking on his cock." She pantomimed the accompanying gesture. "I could tell he was getting close," she continued, doing a gesture of either his penis getting longer or turning into a eggplant.

People had started watching. Sally was blushing. The rest of us had a buzz and didn't care.

"I had told him before... I don't swallow that shit. It is gross!" She made a face like she tasted something horrible.

Tears streamed down my face. "And?"

"Then, instead of telling me he was about to blow his load in my face," she continued, still gesturing wildly. I seriously was going to pee myself if she continued much longer. "He just fucking did it! Came right there in my mouth. Fucking Asshole."

It took me a moment to catch my breath before I could ask. "Wait... I thought you said you *accidentally swallowed*?" I air quoted with my fingers.

"Oh! Yes! I did. Because I should have spit it out, but then I swallowed it and almost puked!" She said this as if she were reciting an especially important fact.

"How is that an accident?" Sally can't drink, so as the sober one, she was laughing like crazy.

"Because I didn't mean to!" Amber didn't understand why we were laughing so hard.

"So, you meant to spit but swallowed the cum instead?" This time Sally asked it as if sorting out facts in a puzzle.

"Yep. Total accident. It was horrible." She nodded seriously in confirmation.

"Why are you fighting about this again?" Alex asked. I was surprised she had taken so long to jump on this bandwagon.

"Because he is an asshole," Amber declared.

"Ahh... I think we need another round," I said, turning toward the bar.

John stood there. "Champagne?"

How Many Shots to Forget This Happened?

"Are you okay?" John asked, setting up some shot glasses on the bar.

"You are not giving us champagne shots, are you?" I smiled and winked, trying to recover from what I am sure was a shocked look on my face.

I am not sure why I was surprised. He worked there. As I watched him pour very colorful shots which he topped with a cherry, I wondered why I was truly freaking out. Can't I make out with a guy in a storeroom and not have it get weird?

"So, what are you doing later?" he asked, sliding the shots across the bar toward me.

This is why you can't make out with a bartender in a storeroom at a club you want to frequent.

"Not sure." I nodded in the direction of the girls. "It's a birthday night, so it depends on what the birthday girl wants."

He smiled. "Let me know if you want to hang out later." He gestured at the shots. "Those are on me."

Phew! That turned out to be much easier than I thought.

Famous last words.

The night continued with shots and dancing.

Sally, Lucy, and Alex left around 1am, leaving Baley and me to babysit our now super-drunk friend.

It was just a little over an hour and several more shots later that Amber's ex/current boyfriend walked up to us on the dance floor.

"Hey Babe," he said leaning in for a kiss.

Amber backed away. "What in the *FUCK* are you doing here?" This was said with a lot more slurring.

"You texted me?" I'm not sure why this sounded like a question. He stared at her.

"No, I didn't! You're a fucking asshole!" She was super drunk. I was drunk, but she was super drunk.

*Whore Tip: Never drunk dial. It is a horrible idea
and never, never, NEVER ends well.*

He pulled out his phone and held it up. "You sent me this!"

I could tell Amber was trying to focus on the phone but unable to.

I leaned in. The text read:

"Mizzz u! Come git ne! At boom rooooom! NoW!"

"What's it say?" she asked, looking at me with squinted eyes.

I sighed. "It says you wanted him to come get you."

"I did?"

"That's what it says."

"Oh. Why did I do that?" she asked, confused.

This was not going to end well no matter what.

"Are you ready to go home?" I asked hopefully. Baley was nodding her head in agreement.

"It's my birthday!" Amber's arms flailed in the air.

"We know." I gently guided her arms back down. We were drawing attention for several reasons now, the first being that we were standing in the middle of the dance floor not dancing.

"Okay. Let's get a shot," she said, heading toward the bar.

As the ex/current BF turned to follow, I grabbed his arm. "You're sober?"

He nodded. "Yeah."

Since Amber had hit the sloppy drunk level of the evening, leaving her with someone sober who cared for her, who came when she asked, seemed like the best choice. This was also because I was in drunkville myself.

> *Whore Tip: Sloppy drunk is not attractive on anyone!*
> *Learn your limit and stay just under it if nothing else.*

I let him go and caught up with Amber. "Sweetie, me and Baley are heading out. We love you!" I leaned in for a hug goodbye and Baley followed suit.

Amber hugged us back. "I love you bitches!"

Heading toward the door with Baley calling a ride, I thought we were heading toward a good night's sleep.

Just as we stepped outside the door into the night air, I heard a voice say, "Leaving without even saying goodbye?" I turned to see my bartender walking up, arms outstretched as if prepping for a hug. I hugged him back.

"Sorry. Just late I guess," I said as he stepped back.

"I just got off. Wanna grab a coffee?" Looking at him, I remembered how gorgeous he was without his shirt on.

I glanced at Baley who just smiled as her ride pulled up. "Call me when you get home," she said, hugging me.

"I will. Let me know when you are home." She nodded and got into the car.

John wrapped his arm around my waist and guided me toward his car which was around back behind the bar. This sounded a little sketchy, but half the bar parking was located around the back.

The car he drove was a Jeep. I took a picture of the back of it and texted it to Baley. John just laughed and opened the door for me.

When I got in, I found that there were a lot of papers at my feet. It was dark, and I couldn't make out what they were at first. When he started the car and the interior lights came on, I noticed that they were food wrappers.

I was too drunk for red flags. I rolled down the window, and he started driving.

We pulled up to a Dunkin' Donuts drive thru, and he asked me what I wanted. I ordered a large light and sweet.

As he handed me my coffee, he asked if I wanted to hang out for a bit. Drunk me agreed and he drove us to his place. He was still super cute. I thought about his fingers sliding inside me again and couldn't help but start to get wet.

He lived in a duplex.

"What street is this?" I asked as I got out of the Jeep, trying to balance my coffee and my phone.

"What?" He looked a little confused.

"Your street names?" I gestured toward the road.

"Drew?"

"Drew Street?"

"Yes."

I sent the building number, which was on the front, and the street to Baley. It would occur to me the next day that I didn't know what city we had been in, but we had not driven far.

As we entered his apartment, I saw it was smaller than it looked from the outside. He had a living room with a little kitchenette. There was a small bedroom and a bathroom.

I set my purse and phone down on the counter in the kitchen. There were dirty dishes in the sink. Before I could discover more, he came up behind me and spun me around, kissing me hard. I almost spilled my coffee.

"Wait," I said, pulling back a little and putting my cup down.

I put my finger on his lips. "Hold that thought," I told him, and I moved toward the bathroom.

When I got inside, I fumbled for the light. I found it and sat down to pee looking for the toilet paper. It was a mostly used up roll sitting on the sink. I finished up, washed my hands with a bar of soap from the shower, and headed back out.

He was not in the living room anymore, and he called, "In here, Gorgeous." I followed the sound to the bedroom and found him on the bed, undressed and covered only slightly with a sheet. There were piles of clothes and soda cans strewn around the room.

"You should join me." He smiled and patted the bed next to him.

I started to slowly undress. He watched me remove every piece of clothing. His smile just got wider.

"God, you're even more gorgeous with your clothes off," he said, throwing the sheet off his lap.

Looking at him aroused made goosebumps breakout all over my skin. He was thick, and since this was the first time really seeing him, all of him, I was impressed.

He had a slight six pack on his abs, broad shoulders, and nice legs.

Whore Tip: If you are working out, remember to focus on all the parts of you. It is terrible when your top half doesn't match your bottom half.

"So... Hot Stuff... What do you have in mind?" I placed my hands on my hips, slightly tilting them and watching his eyes follow my moves.

"I want to lick your peach." He licked his lips.

I moved over toward the bed. I knew because of my state of inebriation that I was not nearly as graceful as I thought.

He laid all the way down on the bed and gestured for me to straddle his face. While a little surprising, I was more than willing to assume the position. As I did, his arms grabbed hold of my legs.

I felt his tongue lick the length of my folds, and I placed my hands on the wall to hold on. There was no headboard or frame for that matter, just wall, but when he began to suck on my core, I just closed my eyes and let myself be pleasured.

He knew how to touch every part of me to send waves of pleasure. His tongue was gentle, and I barely felt it. Other times he was more forceful, and I would feel his tongue part my lips and slide inside me.

My moans grew louder, and with every single one, he sucked and licked harder. Then the tingles raced up my body, and I began to tremble. I screamed as I came all over his face.

After a moment of catching my breath, I moved off his face and he grabbed a towel off the floor to wipe his face. "You taste like candy."

"Well, I am a sweetheart." I smiled back.

"Lay with me," he said, assuming the big spoon position.

I laid down beside him, using his arm as a pillow, and he cuddled close. I could still feel his erect cock pressing against me. I anticipated him sliding inside of me, but he began gently kissing down my neck and shoulders and running his fingers down my back, hips, and thighs.

I closed my eyes as I heard him humming, and then I did the sexiest thing in the world. I fell asleep.

I woke because I felt something moving next to me. I rolled over and opened my eyes to find John lying next to me, on his back, masturbating. I met his gaze, and he smiled, and I was not sure exactly what I should do. This wasn't a getting himself primed motion or a watch me as I pleasure myself.

He was going at it as if I wasn't there.

Then I noticed a scent. Actually, it was more of an odor. As I looked around to see where it might be coming from, I noticed it was stronger closer to the bed. I leaned down, trying to be discreet, but the smell was like wet body odor. I cringed. He continued with his activities.

I sat up then because I find once I acknowledged the smell it just got stronger. I am sure this is a mental thing. I looked down at the sheets and they were dirty. I looked around the room with the light now streaming in from the window and realized this place was filthy.

This was a case of environment beer googles. I stood up; he was just finishing. I noticed he came all over his own stomach and then grabbed the towel he used to clean his face to wipe it up. I was gathering my clothes which were sitting on top of cans, clothes, food wrappers, and other things when he finally spoke.

"Where are you going? I was just getting started."

I looked over to find him reclining on the bed, his dick in his hand again.

"I have to go." I slid on my shoes and headed toward my purse.

The rest of the apartment was the same level of filth as the bedroom. I grabbed my purse and found my phone. I had never found the Lyft app so fast in my life and ordered a car. It said it would be twelve minutes.

I really had to pee and thought that since I had done it last night, I could at least do that again. When I opened the bathroom door, the smell of urine and moldy clothes hit my nose. I couldn't pee in here.

How drunk was I last night? John was still cute by the morning light, but god, how had I missed all this?

"When can I see you again?" he hollered from the bedroom.

He wasn't even getting up to see me out. Maybe that wasn't a terrible thing.

I opened the front door; it hadn't been locked. That was super safe.

I decided to wait outside, trying not to think about my bladder.

I texted Baley. "Heading home. So gross. Details later."

When the car arrived, I was super happy to find that I was only six minutes from my house. I was out of the car the moment it stopped in front of my house. I raced into the bathroom and pulled my pants off, finally feeling relief. It was short lived because I could smell John's place all over me.

I got in the shower right after for as long as the water would run warm and then washed the clothes I had been wearing.

So, when assessing the situation, I was happy John did not have my number. I had never texted after he gave me his. I was less happy that I would not be able to go to that bar anytime soon.

Whore Tip: Never regret your mistakes. Just try not to repeat them.

14

Vampire or Prey

I t was about two weeks later when we decided to have brunch on Sunday morning. There was a restaurant that specialized in pancakes, one of the most important feel-good food groups as far as I was concerned.

I decided on the bananas foster pancakes. Alex chose ones with a berry compote and loads of whipped cream. Baley went simple with blueberry.

> *Whore Tip: Ensure you make time with your friends.*
> *Creating memories is most likely the best thing you*
> *will ever acquire.*

We were almost finished when we got a group text from Sally: "What are you guys doing next Saturday night?"
We all looked up at each other.
"Should we mess with her?" I offered.
Alex shook her head, giggling a little.
"Why?" Baley replied to the text.
Sally: "Two words my friends: Vampire Ball."
"Vampire Ball?" Baley asked, looking at us.
"I'm in," I typed back.
"Me 2," Baley replied.

"Did you actually just use the number two instead of typing the extra character?" Alex's eyes narrowed slightly. "Yes, I am judging you," she said, then began typing on the phone.

"How fancy is this ball?" Alex was more logical and less impulsive.

"I doubt it is an actual ball…" I realized as the words left my lips that this in fact could be an actual ball. Sally would be totally into something like that.

Alex took a sip of her coffee.

I ended up typing back: "This isn't an actual 'ball,' is it?" I narrowed an eye at Alex.

It only took a moment for Sally to send a picture of the flyer for the event. It was a Vampire Ball at a bar in Saint Petersburg where you were supposed to dress as either a vampire or a victim. That was an easy decision.

We were all in. In total, eight of us decided to go. Amber was up for it. We all made the mental note not to let her drink too much this time. Of course, that was slightly hypocritical of me because of John. Just thinking his name made me cringe. Yuck.

By the time Saturday night rolled around, we had all decided between vampire and prey. I was a vampire. I chose a black lace up corset, black jeans, and knee-high black boots. Of course, we also purchased fangs for this occasion. Not the cheesy plastic kind. We got the ones that adhered to your canine teeth. We would put Dracula to shame.

We decided to drive together. The event was at PUSH, a three-story bar. The bottom floor had live music and an open courtyard. It was very New Orleans. The middle was a hip-hop club with two bars and the top floor was an open terrace with a bar, cigar bar, and lounge seating.

As we entered the second floor, we found it had been done up as a vampire's lair. The drink specials were all themed around blood, and the bartenders were dressed up as prey (aka servants).

The place was pretty packed with people: some dressed as if they were at a real ball, some in theme clothes like us, and others that were just enjoying the vampires around them.

Approaching the bar, I scanned the room to find any potential prey. Alex walked up beside me and pointed near the VIP section, some large booths roped off where you could pay for bottle service.

Whore Tip: There are way better ways to spend your money on a night out with friends than bottle service.

Standing on the edge of the dance floor was a tall blonde drink of water. He wore a white t-shirt that highlighted his chiseled features. With a glass in his hand, he surveyed all that was before him. He also had a couple of hot girls in the booth with him and his friends.

I smiled at Alex. "Maybe later if I am hungry."

We both laughed, got drinks, and headed to the dance floor.

The music was amazing, and we shook our money makers. At various times, guys would move in and out of our group. Some tested to see if we were interested. Some assumed we were and had to be shooed away. Others would appear behind one of us trying to grind. I called this particular breed of club inhabitant the "Denim Penis."

If you can't already imagine why we call them this, then you have never felt a guy grind up behind you, pushing their man bits into your butt with only the fabric holding them back.

The music and drinks continued. Although the theme for the night should have been perfect for hunting. it turned out to be perfect for simply having a fun time with friends.

At one point, I was grinding to the beat of an especially dirty song. You know the kind that is a perfect beat to have sex to? I felt someone come up behind me, place his hand on my hip, and begin to dance.

Alex was in front of me, and I did Big Eyes to see if my reaction should be pleased or pissed. She smiled and nodded a little. By her reaction, I could tell I shouldn't disengage from this particular partner. Continuing to dance, I moved to entice him to follow.

Whore Tip: If you are dancing at a club, let the girl lead with her movements. If you are dancing at a wedding, let the guy lead until after the chicken dance.

The next song started to play, and I used this moment to turn to see who my would-be Denim Penis was attached to.

It was hot blonde guy from the booth.

"Well hello," I said into his ear.

"Hello back," he responded.

We continued dancing for another song until he leaned in and asked me to join him at the booth.

There is an unspoken language among friends, if they are good ones, where with just a couple of nods and winks I let them know I was going where he was leading me.

My new friend led me into the booth to meet his friends. They had apparently ordered three different bottles: Vodka, Rum, and Tequila. They also had a supply of mixers like juice and soda.

Because of my buzzed state at this moment in the evening I will call his boothmates by their nicknames:

Bald One: he was attractive and short, and his button-down shirt had enough buttons open to see his ample chest hair, aka Tony.

Pouty One: my first impression was he was brooding, but then after sitting next to him for a bit, I realized he was just not happy with life. He was pretty attractive in a Penn Badgley sort of way. His name was Ryan.

Slimy One: he was full of flattery at first, had all the right lines, perfect smile, but when you were around him for more than a few minutes, you felt like you needed a shower. He had a name, but I think we will just call him Slug.

As I sat down in the booth, the Slug poured me a drink of vodka and cranberry before asking. Now some might consider this a sweet gesture. However, they had several options, and it would have taken only moments to ask.

Bald one asked me what my name was.

"Randi," I replied, smiling and taking the drink.

I took it, then looked over at the sexy blonde man. I leaned in to him and asked, "So what name should I be screaming out later?" This might have been the drinks or the corset making me feel like a predator.

> *Whore Tip: Own how you feel. Get your confidence where you find it. You only need to impress yourself.*

He smiled. "Randy."

"Your name is Randy? How perfect!"

He smiled again and took another drink before grabbing my hand and leading me to the dance floor.

We danced and drank. He was so amazingly hot. As his hands explored me as we danced, I felt heat flow through me, and my nipples hardened. Grinding against him, I felt his stiff shaft through his jeans, and I knew he wanted me as much as I wanted him.

After a time, he asked if I wanted to "hang out" for a bit. This was after Pouty One came and whispered something into this ear. I nodded, leaning in to let him know I would just let my friends know.

I made my way over to where Alex was at the bar. She was laughing and talking to Amber. When I asked where the others were, she nodded in the direction of the dance floor. I scanned and found that Sally and Baley together in the middle of the floor. The moment I made eye contact with Baley, she did Big Eyes, so I made my way over to her.

When I got closer, I saw that Sally snickered as a noticeably short man held Baley's left hand. She was trying to pull away and he kept trying to whisper something to her. I grabbed her hand away from him and smiled as I pulled her in the direction of the bar.

When we got there, Baley thanked me. "You won't believe what he just said to me," she smiled and started laughing.

I took the bait. "What?"

"Well..." she started. "When he asked if I wanted to dance by grabbing my hand and pulling me to him, I politely said 'Thank you but I am married' and he looked at my ring and said, 'I could suck the diamond right out of your ring!'" Sally was laughing so hard with her that there were tears coming out of their eyes at this point. "I had to tell him that would not make me any less married and then you showed up. The end!"

"That is truly amazing," Amber said raising her glass.

"Guy logic is precious." Alex bumped her glass against Amber's.

All of the sudden, the girls stopped laughing. They were looking behind me. I turned and it was Randy.

"Oh," I smiled, then turned back to the girls. "We're going to go 'hang out'... You know... together." I hoped he couldn't see the smirk on my face.

I know Sally wanted to say something but stopped herself.

Alex walked up and whispered something to Randy. He said something back. She pulled out her phone and started typing. She said something back to him and smiled at me.

"Make good choices," Amber said as Randy led me away, and I watched as he pulled his phone out looking at a text. Alex was looking out for me, and for a brief moment, I wondered what she would be like if she used her powers for evil instead of good. It was a scary thought.

Whore Tip: Make good choices! ☺

15

Not Making
Good Choices

L eaving the club, it turned out that the boys had all driven together. That meant that I ended up squeezing in the back-seat of Bald One's Charger between Randy and Pouty One.

"Do those come out?" Randy asked, pointing at my lips. It was in this moment that I remembered that my vampire fangs were still in place. I licked one of them seductively. "What makes you think they are not mine?" I said with a wink which caused him to smile back at me.

The problem was that these were pretty fancy fake fangs that came with a particular adhesive which meant they would stay in place until I soaked them off with a salty warm water concoction. Basically, they were not coming off anytime soon. I was going to have to make this vamp roleplay work for the rest of the evening.

When we finally arrived at the house, both Slug and Bald One headed out, saying their goodbyes and a couple of terribly cheesy jokes to Randy hoping they didn't find him dead from bleeding, but if they did, it would be worth it.

When we walked inside, Pouty One followed us.

At first, I wondered what was happening. The very inebriated me thought that I might be getting my first threesome, and I had to say this was the hottest of his friends so I thought I could be down for it.

I started to run through how it would work and if Randy here was going to ask or just assume it was fine with me. All of these scenarios played through my head along with several others until we walked in the door and the Pouty One turned down a hallway saying, "Night Guys."

That was not as naughty as it should have been. When I looked over at my new playmate, he simply stated, "He's my roommate."

I excused myself to the bathroom to freshen up a bit and get my head in the game so to speak. The bathroom was much cleaner than I thought it would be. I decided as I was drying my hands on a clean hand towel that this must be part of the quirks of Pouty Roommate.

The lights were all out when I opened the door, and there were candles lit. I made my way down the hallway and ended up in the doorway of his bedroom. He was lighting another candle on his dresser. He turned and said, "I thought vampires might like it better in the dark," and set down the lighter, stalking toward me.

He pulled me toward him with one arm and shut the door with the other. When his lips met mine, they were soft and forceful. He tasted a little like whiskey, and I pulled his white t-shirt from his jeans and slid my hands up his shirt, almost clawing at him, and then it happened...

When I had decided on being a vampire for the evening, I found a set of fangs called "love bites" (They are made by Scarecrow) and they were a good size so my mouth could close easily. Trust me: this is a concern when you are wearing fangs. Another even more major concern is making sure they stay in place. Because I knew I would be drinking and dancing, possibly even a little biting, I did not want them falling out. I used the special adhesive to keep them exactly where they were.

So, I just accidentally, but for real, bit him.

I wasn't sure if this killed the mood, but he spun me and pushed me toward the bed instead.

Another logistical situation was the lace up knee-high boots and the corset. The corset was laced up in the back, but it had little hooks in the front. I hooked it onto myself and then Baley tightened it into place with the laces. Voila! Curvy vampire.

I debated leaving it on, but only for a moment as he removed the remaining clothing he had on. He was something off the cover of a steamy romance cover with muscles in all the right places.

As fast as I could, I popped the hooks and my breasts broke free. He just watched, and I bent over and unlaced my shoes, pulling them off along with my jeans. This whole outfit was not very conducive to a night of frolicking.

I slid off my socks as I stood before him in only the thong I had worn that night. As much as I had envisioned how watching me disrobe could be incredibly alluring, I am sure the fumbling and yanking was anything but. However, when I looked at him, he was positively ready for me. His cock stood at attention. Moving toward him, I grasped his shaft in my hand while pulling his lips to my mouth.

The kissing and stroking began gently at first. We tasted each other, finding how our tongues intertwined, but as his hands began to explore my breasts, his fingers found my nipples and he tugged... hard. I almost yelped, not ready for the change in pacing. This was all the encouragement that he needed. He moved me back toward the bed, and as my knees bent, he laid me down, moving so he was kneeling over me. He looked like a predator.

He pushed my arms above my head as his mouth kissed and licked my neck, and as he reached my collarbone, he nibbled, and I began to wonder who was the vampire and who was the prey.

Whore Tip: Be willing to switch roles. You will find the right combination for any encounter.

He moved down my body, licking and nibbling. Goosebumps erupted all over my skin as he took my breasts in each of his hands and used his tongue to circle my nipples. Heat built between my thighs. My thong was soaked already.

I felt his weight moving off the bed as he spread my legs, kneeling between them. His warm wet lips kissed up my inner thighs. His breath teased my skin as he slid his hands up, grabbing ahold of my thong and pulling it down.

Because my legs were parted, he couldn't move it beyond a certain point. I looked down toward him, and he got a wicked grin as he ripped the fabric, throwing the thong across the room.

He lifted my legs onto his shoulders, placing his hands onto my thighs. I leaned back again, feeling his mouth so close to my wetness.

He licked from the bottom of my folds, plunging his tongue into me as deep as he could go, and his nose touched my hood, sending shivers throughout me.

As he hungrily lapped me up, I felt my legs start to tremble and my hands instinctively reached up for something to hold on to, and under the pillow at the top of the bed, my fingers closed around something cold.

His tongue hit just the right spot causing and orgasm to ripple through me. My back arched and a grabbed hold of the sheets as he held me to his mouth and continued to suck.

I rolled with a second orgasm and was almost thrashing trying to remove my legs from his grip. Wishing this were more dignified but I was too sensitive, and he didn't want to let up.

I moved my arms up again hoping to grab on to something, anything. My hand hit whatever cold, solid object was under the pillow, and it went sailing off the bed, hitting the wall hard and landing on the floor.

This sudden noise startled both of us, and he let go, quickly moving over to see what had hit the wall.

Sitting up on the bed, I watched as he leaned over. "Oh shit," he said, grabbing something off the floor.

"Okay. Don't freak out," he said in what I am sure he thought was a calming tone. One thing I have learned, however, is those are the words that can almost guarantee that a person would freak out. Sitting naked on the bed, I was sure I was not prepared for whatever he was about to show me.

He turned around, and in his hand was a gun.

Yep. That is right. It was a gun. A 9mm to be exact.

He quickly moved to put the gun in the top drawer of the dresser, and I kept my eyes on him the entire time.

In case you are wondering, a gun being thrown across the room is a very sobering moment.

Returning to bed, he sat beside me. Since I had never been in this situation before, I knew that the look on my face was probably confusion at best.

"Umm," he began. "So, I am sorry about that."

I wasn't sure if an apology was warranted. Moreover, the apology told me that he hadn't planned on a hook-up tonight, or minimally, he did not have a lot of confidence in his ability to make that happen.

> *Whore Tip: Remember to look at things from all perspectives. This way you can find the ray of light. If there is one.*

"You don't have to apologize." I smiled at him. His face showed that he was nervous. I wondered if he thought that I might bolt out of the room. This would have been a more likely if I was not currently naked and covered in my own cum, although the drama of grabbing my clothes and bolting down the hall made me smirk.

"Don't worry, sexy. I am just disappointed for the interruption." He smiled a little at that, running his fingers through his hair. He stood up, grabbing some shorts off the floor. "Want something to drink?" he asked.

"Water," I replied, and he nodded and headed out of the room.

So, I can say this was an absolute first for me. I thought for a bit, but knew we could not recover this here in this room. If there was any hope of reciprocating for the amazing orgasms, I would have to change venues.

When he returned, I had my jeans on, stuffing my thong in my pocket, and was finishing buttoning up the corset, which was not an easy task. He handed me a glass of water, taking a slow sip out of another he carried for himself.

After a moment of somewhat awkward silence, I asked, "Give me a ride home?"

He smiled, swallowed the last of his water, put on his jeans again, and grabbed a clean shirt.

The drive home was mostly silent. We did discuss vampires, the apparent theme of the night, how it was actually Brooding Friend's idea to go out tonight, and how Randy was a nurse in real life.

It was a super polite conversation. I gave directions when I needed to, and he turned on music. I stared out the window and wondered how I could spin this back to the direction I wanted it to go, which, of course, was back to us being naked.

As he pulled up in my driveway, I decided I had to make my move. "I was wondering..." I smirked a little as I met his gaze, "if you would help me carry my phone inside?"

A glimmer of confusion crossed his face, and then he smiled at me again. "Absolutely!"

When I opened the door, I began removing my corset again, anticipating he was following me. When it was undone, I simply threw it aside and entered the bedroom. I put one hand on the wall and removed my boots. Finally, after pulling my jeans down, I turned around.

He had a smile on his face as he dropped his jeans to the floor next to the shirt he had discarded.

Moving up to him, I ran my hands up his chest until I could fist his hair in my hand, and I brought his mouth to mine. This time I was not as gentle.

I wanted him and again his body told me he wanted me as well. Still kissing him, I turned him so we began moving back toward the bed. When we reached the edge, I pushed him down on his back and climbed on top of him.

He moved himself up on the bed, bringing more of his body, and I moved with him, licking as well as kissing.

When he was finally settled, I leaned over to the nightstand, grabbed a condom, and unwrapped it, sliding it on his hard cock. He watched my every movement.

Sliding him inside me, I felt him expand my tight walls. Rocking my hips forward, I moved up and down on his hard shaft. His mouth met mine again, our tongues chasing each other as my nerve center rubbed against him with every thrust.

I pulled back to sit on him, my back arching as I came. I tried to maintain my movements as tremors of ecstasy flowed through me. As if sensing my wavering ability to maintain the rhythm, he placed his hands on my hips, guiding me to move faster and pushing himself deeper into me with every thrust.

I began to come again, and his cock pulsed. He held on to me as we both rode through the orgasm to completion.

His hands moved from my hips, and I moved to lay next to him, still panting.

"Wow," he finally said, between ragged breaths.

> *Whore Tip: It is always a good thing when you find that someone can take your breath away.*

"Super wow," I agreed.

After a little rest, he moved to stand up. "Down the hall," I said, smiling and pointing. He smiled back and headed down the hall to the bathroom.

I grabbed a towel and cleaned myself off a little as I heard the door open, and he returned to the room. I moved back to the bed where he laid down again.

He pulled me to him and kissed me again. It was nice just lying there, enjoying the moment. I wondered if we would go for another round, and as his fingertips caressed my side, I knew I was fine even if this was the only time.

I wasn't sure how many hours had passed when I woke up still in his arms. He was asleep. I tried to fall back asleep, but I knew I needed to pee. I tried to quietly move out of the room.

When I returned, he was awake and pulling on his jeans.

"Sorry I crashed." His voice had a weird tone.

"I did, too. No worries," I replied. He wasn't really making eye contact now. It took me a moment to realize what was going on. He did not want the falling asleep in each other's arms to mean anything. We had never discussed the rules. I was sure he had run into the situation where women had read more into the situation then he intended. I was even more sure he had not figured out how to deal with it yet.

I stood up and threw on a shirt and shorts.

"Thanks again for the ride," I said, winking as I made my way toward the door.

As I opened the door, he said, "It was nice to meet you, Randi."

"It was nice to meet you as well, Randy," I said.

He paused. "You know my name is Aaron, right?" His tone was a mixture of playfulness and concern.

"Yep, yep, yep, yep," I blurted. "Just messing with you." I had no idea how to recover. He kissed my cheek, and I waved goodbye.

Whore Tip: Try to call your playmate by the right name unless they request otherwise.

When I told Alex the next day what had happened, she only laughed, then told me to call Sally (who worried I might have been abducted). I did call, although I left the part out about the gun. She would not see the humor the same way Alex did.

16

MR. BIG – TAKE ONE

I can say that after meeting Aaron, yes, I remember his name now, that I needed to return to my familiar hunting grounds—online—versus getting drunk at a club and going home with a gun-toting nurse. Although, that would make a ridiculously awesome Tarantino movie.

It was a Thursday evening when I received a message online. It said:

> "Good Evening,
>
> *This may seem a bit forward, but I felt if I did not attempt to reach out to you, it might turn into one of those regrets later. I am a successful architect who enjoys good music, good wine, and an enchanting woman. I see you are not looking for something too serious. My schedule would not permit it anyhow.*
>
> *Hoping I piqued your interest,*
>
> *Ed."*

This could possibly be the most polite message I have ever received. Of course, it did in fact pique my interest.

Scrolling through his profile, I found he only had a couple photos and minimal information. For those fans of *Sex in The City*, Ed looked like Mr. Big with a goatee.

I sent him back a quick reply. "You have my attention. Tell me more."

> *Whore Tip: Do not overthink responses. Sometimes being cute and witty is all you need.*

The next day I got a reply. It turned out he lived in Sarasota, which for those of you unfamiliar with Florida was approximately an hour south from where I lived. Now if you visited *My Home on Whore Island*, you know a drive is not a big deal. Ronnie, whom I still occasionally played with, also lived in that area.

The thought crossed my mind that I could possibly make it a two-for-one visit and see both Ronnie and Ed in the same weekend. Ronnie never minded when I crashed at his apartment when I came down his way; in fact, he encouraged it because we were able to go several rounds before I headed home.

> *Whore Tip: There is absolutely nothing wrong with having multiple partners in close timing or even at the same time if you are all on the same page as to what is going on.*

As we continued to chat via email, Ed let me know he had a mid-size architectural firm. He also told me that he had recently gotten a divorce and was amazed he had found someone like me. On the surface, it sounded like I had found another potential playmate.

Our interactions quickly moved from email to phone calls and texts. He was alluring in a very gentlemanly way. Don't get me wrong: he was very naughty when he wanted to be. But unlike some of the more crass or blunt playmates I have had, he would caress me with his words.

His voice was deep and husky. I found myself constantly anticipating meeting him.

His insane work schedule caused our first meeting to be rescheduled several times. He would apologize several times and promise not to miss the next one. At first, this was a cute quality, an executive letting go and making time to spend a few hours with me. He would tell me how much he "needed this time" away from the hectic life he led. After the third time, however, this idea lost a lot of the appeal.

Part of the reason I set up casual interactions is because, for the most part, there are no negative emotions. My last actual relationship had been destroyed because he had cheated on me.

When you get cheated on, you find that even though the reason a person cheats has almost nothing to do with you and almost everything to do with them, you still end up wondering what you did wrong and why this could possibly happen to you.

That relationship broke my willingness to put my emotions on the line again. Jessie had also given me a reminder about not letting a person too close to me in the feelings department.

Ed wanted to meet at a martini bar near his office. I had looked into the place when he had suggested it. It was in a very fancy resort hotel on the beach. It was a bar for people in suits or cocktail attire from their conferences held in the hotels nearby.

I had been excited to pull out one of my little black dresses, put my hair up, and created a carefully constructed make-up look.

However, Ed now found a chink in the armor. He texted saying that he could not take it again. When I put in the effort to get ready and drive to a location that makes it easier on him to meet, I am making myself vulnerable.

I dialed Sally's number, but hung up before it rang. I knew she would be sweet and sympathetic, but I did not need that now. I needed not to spiral because this wasn't worth it.

*Whore Tip: When you spot a trigger, recognize it,
how it happens, and how to avoid it if possible. We
all have them; it is what you do with that knowledge
that makes all the difference.*

I called Baley. She answered right away. "I thought you would
be knee deep in Mr. Big land by now."

Baley loved *Sex in the City* and agreed with the nickname I had
given him.

"He cancelled," I said, hearing the frustration in my own voice.

"He did what? Never mind. I ignore that. Where are you now?"
She seemed a little concerned. It seemed that the tone of my voice
was crystal clear to her as well.

"I am most of the way to Sarasota," I replied.

"Sarasota?"

"Yes."

"So, what about a back-up plan?" There was a playfulness
to her tone.

"Back up plan?" I was confused.

"Tall... green eyes..." She was leading me there. "...working on
truth... justice..."

"Ronnie?" I asked, wondering why I had not thought to text him.
Normally we made plans a week or so out, but what could it hurt?

"Brilliant!" was my reply.

"You're welcome. Keep me posted." She hung up.

I texted Ronnie to see what he was up to that evening. He was
working, but was excited that I would be in his apartment when
he got home.

Negative feelings gone, I drove with renewed anticipation.

Whore Tip: It is not a bad idea to have a back-up plan.

17

THE BACK-UP PLAN

Ronnie was one of my favorite playmates because he understood the rules. They fit into his lifestyle and mine perfectly. He was a law student who worked as a waiter in a fancy restaurant. He also had one of the most perfect penises I had ever had the opportunity to penetrate me.

As I drove into Sarasota, I knew I had a couple of hours before Ronnie would be off from work, and although I knew how to get into his apartment beforehand, and I would, I had not eaten yet and did not bring my normal overnight kit.

Most nights with Ronnie lead to overnight stays. Since I did not plan on staying with Ed that night, I had not brought my normal overnight bag and only had my Just-In-Case case.

> *Whore Tip: A Just-In-Case case is a vital tool for all. It should contain: condoms of varying sizes, lube, breath mints, and moist towelettes (or baby wipes in a pinch). This way you are prepared no matter what happens.*

I drove to a Target and grabbed a toothbrush, a bottle of wine, and some clothes for the drive back tomorrow. I wondered if I should change out of the little black dress outfit. This was that little inner voice that did not want to have to explain why I was all dressed up already. Conveniently for me, this little voice was also overthinking it.

Ronnie was a playmate, not a boyfriend or even someone I would put in the category of dating. He wouldn't care why I was dressed the way I was. For our first encounter, I was dressed up like a naughty schoolgirl, so this could just be another enticing way to steam up our encounter.

> *Whore Tip: If you are not in a relationship, the only person you owe an explanation to is yourself. Do not worry what another is thinking; it should have no bearing on your choices.*

One of the wonderful parts about living on the coast in Florida was that we had some of the best seafood restaurants. I sent my pick-up order to one near Ronnie's apartment and grabbed it on the way.

When I got into this apartment, I found the wine opener, poured myself a glass, and enjoyed my dinner and the rest of the bottle of wine in anticipation of having him for dessert.

Ronnie arrived earlier than I thought he would. When I heard the front door open, I stood up. He came into the living room with a smile on his face that only widened when he laid his eyes on me.

"Wow," he said and gently bit down on his lower lip.

I walked over to where he was standing and laid my hands on his chest, tilting my head so my lips hovered right in front of his.

"Wow is right," I whispered as my tongue slid out to touch his lips.

His mouth opened for me and his tongue met mine. He lips were warm, and we tasted each other. Pulling back from me, he said, "I need to shower off work, but you look so delicious I think I have to have a taste."

He placed a bag he was holding down on the table and knelt in front of me. Running his hands up my thighs until his fingers hooked around the sides of my panties, he pulled them down until I stepped out of them, and he cast them to the side.

He grabbed my calves and tugged, indicating I should spread them a little wider. I obliged, and he started planting kisses starting at my knees. Warm breath caressed my skin. I closed my eyes and tilted my head back slightly, enjoying every sensation.

I felt his hands move up to my thighs, lifting my dress. He nibbled a little and goosebumps pebbled my skin. I had to bend my knees a little to steady myself. As he neared my already very wet pussy, I started to tremble.

"You smell amazing," he purred and then I felt his lips against mine. He pushed his tongue into the peak of my wetness, rolling the tip in rhythm against my pearl as it swelled. The orgasm began to roll through me. I ran my fingers through his hair, holding on to him as he continued to suck and play, sending me into another orgasm. This time my knees began to give, and he pulled back, holding onto me so I wouldn't fall. He let me ride it until I met his gaze.

"Ready for round two?" he smirked as he stood and led me toward the bathroom.

As he turned on the water in the huge walk-in shower, the steam began to billow. I always enjoyed watching a man remove his clothes and Ronnie was no exception. As he tossed aside his final piece of clothing, I drank him in.

Whore Tip: Never forget to step back and admire the sexiness of your partner. Even if they are not right off a runway, something about them revs your engine.

He was still slightly engorged, and his lips still had the moisture of me on them. He looked at me, raising an eyebrow. "Oh..." I said, looking down at my still clothed state. "I thought you were going to finish the job." He smiled and pulled me toward his muscular frame. His lips met mine as he kissed me, and I could taste myself on him.

The room was getting warmer as his fingers found the zipper of the dress and pulled it down. I let it fall off my shoulders to the floor. His fingers moved to unclasp my bra, and as he did, he pulled his mouth from mine, tugging the straps down my arms until the bra rested on the floor with my dress.

He opened the shower door and placed his hands on my hips, guiding me inside. He placed me under the flowing hot water at first. I pulled the clip that had been holding my hair in place and put it on the little shelf, then tilted my head under the water.

Running his fingers through my hair, he pulled it to the side so he could nibble on the nape of my neck. I ran my hands down his shoulders and arms until I was able to grab hold of his very erect shaft.

I began to stroke using the water as lubricant. Biting my neck harder, he moaned, "Naughty girl," and moved to take my mouth with his again. His urgency intensified as I continued to caress his manhood. He pulled back and his voice was almost a growl. "I want to be inside of you... now!"

I let go of him with one final squeeze, and he moved me around so I faced the wall. He took each one of my hands in his, placing them on the tiles above me. He pulled his hands away, and I moved my legs apart, slightly arching my back.

I felt the tip of him enter me slowly, ensuring I was ready to take him. One of his hands held me in position as he found that I was wet and tight from my previous orgasms. He took his time, slowly pushing deeper inside. When he hit the limit of what I could take, all of his restraint disappeared, and he began to thrust harder and faster inside me.

Holding onto my hips, he pulled me to him while pushing himself deeper. My hands on the wall assisted with the movement. The harder he thrust, the deeper I wanted him inside me.

The heat of the water on my skin and the heat of him against me was sinful and wonderful. Orgasms rolled though me, one after another. His cock swelled in my tightness, and he erupted inside of me, roaring with satisfaction.

Leaning against me, he kissed down my shoulder and then stepped back, pulling himself from me and causing a slight pleasure tremor deep inside me. Giving myself a bit to recover, I leaned against the tile wall, letting my breath steady.

I turned around, and he pulled me in the water with him, kissing me delicately.

"I'm glad you came down." A smile crossed his lips.

"Me too," I said, smiling back.

Whore Tip: Remember that the loss of one opportunity in life can lead to another even bigger opportunity. Take chances and be willing to have plans change.

After the shower, I checked my phone. I realized Sally would want to know what happened with Mr. Big. I had forgotten to tell her that I had a change of plans and the last thing I needed was for her to go full Liam Neeson looking for me if I did not check in.

I had five missed messages and three missed calls. All of them were from Ed.

Seeing this took a little of the euphoria of the night away. I was tempted to read them and listen to the voicemails, but first I sent a message to Sally: *Change of plans. I am at Ronnie's. I will explain tomorrow.*

She texted back: *What happened?*

I would call her on my drive back in the morning. I did not want to get into it now. I was still irritated by the entire situation. When Ed cancelled, he had been brief in his excuse, and all I had said was something along the lines of okay, then hung up.

I decided not to dive into that rabbit hole right now. Ronnie was waiting for round two (or was it three?) and I would rather concentrate on that sensation than the one I would get from reading the texts right now. I needed to be in the right head space, and with it bothering me as much as it still did, I knew this wasn't it.

I sent a quick text to him: *I will chat with you tomorrow*. I put the phone on silent and dropped it in my purse.

"I brought dessert... Interested?" Ronnie said from the kitchen.

"Absolutely," I replied as I let my towel fall to the floor, heading in the direction of the waiting sweetness.

18

Mr. Big – Take Two

I left Ronnie's apartment a little after nine in the morning. He had papers to get done, and I needed a little more sleep than was afforded me being around him. The bliss kept a smile on my face all the way to the car.

It was only after I buckled my seatbelt and started the air-conditioning that I finally read the messages from Ed.

It was apparent that he could sense that I was less than pleased about how this went down. He wanted to make sure that I knew it was not intentional, and that he was sorry for doing this again. That sometimes his work demanded it and that he really did want to meet me. He said he was looking forward to this so much that he became aroused any time he thought about me and that happened at inopportune moments.

Honestly, I was still a little mad. When the car had cooled down—it was Florida after all and summer time, so it was a million degrees outside—I decided to call Sally.

She answered almost immediately. "What the hell happened?"

"Good morning to you as well, Sunshine."

"I'm sorry. Good morning, of course. I have just been wondering what happened all night!" I could tell by her tone that this had been bothering her since I texted.

"It is nothing bad. Well, nothing really bad, I should say." I took a deep breath. "He cancelled... again... at the last minute."

"Are you serious?" This was the type of question that people seem to ask out of habit. I didn't answer and waited for her to continue, which she did without missing a beat.

"How many times is this?"

"Four."

"What are you going to do?" Now her tone was a little more sympathetic.

"I haven't decided yet. It is bothering me too much to make a decision, but I will let you know when I do. As always."

Sally seemed content with this, and we chatted about my night on my way home. She was with me the first time I ever met Ronnie, and since Sally was still secretly hoping that I would meet Prince Charming, I think Ronnie was the one she was rooting for.

After I got home, I took a much-needed nap, made myself a late lunch, and called both Alex and Baley for their advice on what, if anything, to do about Mr. Big.

Alex thought I should just let it go, which I expected, and Baley thought I should let him explain. I didn't like either of these options.

If I needed an explanation, that meant that he affected me beyond a casual play date. I did not want to put myself in that position, even if a small part of me wanted that. On the other hand, I did want to have this experience. He was the first playmate I had chosen that was a powerful executive type. It was a little thrilling.

After watching a few episodes of *Sex in the City*, which I will call homework for this occasion, I decided what I should do. After all, I was much more Samantha than Carrie, and I knew that I had to be in control of this, or it would put me in a weird place emotionally.

I texted him: *I will give this one more chance, but on my terms. Meet me next Saturday night at the Hard Rock Hotel and Casino, L Bar, at 7pm. I will see you then.*

I hoped he understood the role he needed to play. If he did not, then I was sure this was actually done. I was happy his response told me he did: *I will see you there. Can't wait.*

I intentionally had very minimal contact until that night. He texted, but I only gave short replies. I was not mean; I just was not going to put more effort into this than I had decided I was willing to.

> *Whore Tip: Make sure you do a constant check-in with where you are in a situation. You do not owe anyone any more of yourself than you decide to give. If you make the decision on it, there can never be a bad outcome.*

Before I started dressing to meet the elusive Mr. Big, I almost texted to confirm he was arriving. As I started to type, it hit me that I did not actually care if he showed up. If he didn't, I was going to arrive, looking amazing in a hotel that had several bars and plenty of hot guys. There was truly no worry that I could not find a way to occupy my time.

This time I decided to go even more out than last weekend. My dress was a strapless black dress with white polka-dots and a wide red belt that hugged my curves. The make-up was simple, and the hair was pinned at the top with curls falling down my back. Red lips rounded out the look again. I grabbed my purse and headed out.

I left with plenty of time to get there early, but I decided to arrive just a little bit late. I did not want to be the one waiting for him.

When I walked into the bar, there was a little crowd. I started a slow walk around to see if he was there. I did not get far before a waiter approached me. "Are you Randi?"

"I am," I replied with a smirk.

He gestured to the back corner of the room. "Your party is waiting for you."

I looked in the direction he gestured, and sure enough, there was a tall, handsome, broad-shouldered man with a goatee. He looked exactly like his pictures.

I approached the table with a slight swing to my hips. I knew he was watching me. On the table was a chilled bottle of white wine and a cheese plate. It was thoughtful of him.

When I arrived at the table, he stood. Although I was in heels, making me almost six-foot-three, he stood a few inches taller. Reaching out to take my hand, he pulled me closer to him and kissed me on the cheek.

"Please sit," he gestured, and I took a seat.

"You are even more beautiful in person," he said as he looked me up and down.

"I could say the same about you." A slight smile played across my lips. Having stood next to him, I immediately began to think of all the things a man that size could do to and with me. When you are my height, it is not often you find someone who can do all those positions that you only can with someone taller than you.

He reached in and lifted the bottle of wine, showing it to me. I was not familiar with the label, but I held up my glass, and he poured only a little bit as if I was to taste it.

I took a sniff like you are supposed to when sampling wine. Since I was not a wine connoisseur, I had no idea what I was smelling. Don't get me wrong: I do love wine, mainly red and mostly blends, and if you are rolling your eyes right now, I also love a good Malbec, so I am not a total dilettante.

I took a sip. It was dry and crisp. Not one that I would have chosen, but I had no intention of spoiling this mood. I smiled and held my glass out for more.

He filled it and then held his up in a toast. "To new adventures."

"To new adventures," I repeated, clinking glasses.

He was watching my every move closely as I sipped my wine and as I nibbled on the cheese plate. It was not quite predatory; it was as if he was assessing me. Possibly deconstructing my movements. Maybe the architect in him needed to understand how I worked, what made me tick.

Although I had orchestrated the arrival and location, I found the conversation to be lagging. I took another sip of the wine and decided to test the waters a bit. "What are you seeing as you watch me sip the wine?" He smiled and picked up his glass, taking a sip. I noticed his cheeks flushed with a little color. Interesting.

"Do you like the wine?" he replied.

Avoiding.

"It is cool and dry," I answered, taking another sip.

Two can play at this game.

"I picked it because it is one of the best whites they had on the menu." Trying to impress?

"Why is it considered the best?" I was taunting him now, wondering if he would take the bait.

He did.

"The region of…."

I interrupted him before this could get going by placing my finger against my lip, indicating silence.

He stopped speaking and tilted his head, puzzled.

"How prepared for tonight are you exactly?" This time, I downed the rest of my glass in one gulp and gently placed it on the table.

A smile spread across his face. He gestured over to the waiter for the check. I excused myself and told him I would be right back.

The thing about hotels is the bathrooms were not generally located within the bars or restaurants. They were on the hotel floor.

I headed out of the bar without turning around, sure he was watching me. I headed over to the bathroom.

> *Whore Tip: Be confident and willing to control any situation you are in. It might be what takes your adventure from meh to outstanding.*

When I headed back to the bar, he was waiting for me. As I approached, he held out his arm for me to take and then began walking me toward the hotel. I wrapped my hands around his arm and squeezed a little. He was solid, but not muscular like a body builder.

I stole a few glances as we neared the elevator. Knowing he was in his late forties, I could see the white hairs coming through his beard and temples. He turned his head and I did the same. It is, of course, not polite to stare.

When we reached the elevators, he stopped holding my arm and moved his hand to the arch of my back. The doors opened, letting a couple of other guests out, and he urged me to enter, hitting a button for the twelfth floor as the doors closed.

Taking me in his arms, he moved me against the wall of the elevator, kissing my neck. It seemed like time flew as the elevator doors opened, and he pulled away, reaching for my hand and taking it softly in his.

He opened the door to the room and walked inside, holding it open for me to follow. I walked toward the window where the curtains were open.

I felt his breath on my neck as his fingers tugged at the zipper of my dress. I tossed my purse to the chair and undid the belt, letting it fall to the floor where the dress was soon to follow.

I turned, meeting his gaze as my fingers undid the buttons of his shirt and slid it off his shoulders. I could see his pants were having a tough time containing the erection that was growing.

Undoing his belt then button and zipper, I moved to pull pants and boxers to the floor. As I stood up, I turned to face the window again, putting my back toward him.

His fingertips played down my back undoing my strapless bra and letting it fall to the floor. His hands cupped my ass, then he grabbed ahold of the panties pulling them down and kissing down the curve of my lower back then his tongue followed the line between my cheeks to my thighs.

When my panties were down to the floor, I stepped out of them, and he held my legs slightly apart. He moved his hands up my inner thighs, traced his fingers along the wet folds of my pussy, and then slid them inside. It was unexpected but naughty. I rested my hands on the window for support as he pressed his face close, drinking me in. Moving his fingers back out, his tongue tried to get as deep as he moved one hand to hold my hip, pulling me even closer.

Then his tongue moved up and began to lick around my rosebud which caused me to freeze for a moment. Then his free hand moved toward my clit and began to rub. The sensations were amazing, and I wanted more.

I pushed back a little toward him, wanting him to go deeper. This was all the encouragement that he needed, and his tongue slid inside. The heat spread as I began to cum hard. I held on, trying not to move the sensation from both parts of me as one orgasm rolled into another.

My arms were still against the window as he stood, and I felt his fingers slide inside again as my walls continued to pulse with pleasure. Then his fingers moved up to my back door again, sliding in, testing, teasing as he added another and then another, spreading me.

Using my wetness as lubrication, he slowly slid his head inside, and as gentle as he was being, I wanted it harder and rocked back to meet his pushing. It hurt a little but in such a wonderful way.

When he was deep inside me, he held my hips to guide his penetration, moving slowly back and forth. I moved my fingers to rub my clit. It was pure pleasure, and I let myself feel everything as the orgasms rolled one right over one another. His sounds told me how much he wanted everything I was in that moment. His hands held tighter and his thrusts came faster until he finally exploded, roaring as I felt him pulse inside of me.

Time blurred as he pulled out, and I let myself recover. I was not sure I could stand without the assistance of the window.

I heard motion behind me as he moved away, and then came back with a towel, handing it to me. Thanking him, I moved to the bathroom to clean up.

Although anal play is fun, you definitely need a clean up.

> *Whore Tip: If you are 100% into what is going on, it is amazing. If you are not, you always have the option of shutting it down. Only do what you are comfortable with.*

Taking my time, I debated how I wanted my night to end. This encounter was naughty and so amazingly erotic, but I knew that I would need to fully recover.

I opened the bathroom door and found Ed laying in the bed under the covers. I moved over to where my clothes had been cast aside and put them back on.

"Going somewhere?" He leaned into what he was saying. I could tell he wanted me to join him. I smiled as I grabbed my belt and purse and moved over toward the bed. Leaning down, I kissed him deeply.

"Thank you for an amazing evening."

He looked surprised.

"I look forward to doing that again sometime soon," I said with a wink, then I got up and left the room.

As I rode the elevator down to the lobby, I texted Sally that I was on my way back home from a great night. I knew the moment my head hit the pillow, I was going to sleep perfectly.

19

WHAT HAPPENED TO THE FANTASY?

lthough I was happy with how I handled the encounter at the Hard Rock, and Ed told me that he had never had a night like that, things got really weird again quickly.

It started when he texted me the next morning, already wanting to see me again. I was still riding the high from the night before, and when he described the ways he wanted to have me when next we got together, it got me more than a little excited.

However, when I suggested a date and time, he said it wouldn't work with his schedule and he would let me know when he was free next. He never did.

I could understand that, and at first, I figured he was busy.

He would text occasionally, telling me he was thinking of me or remembering how I felt when he was inside of me. It was all very flattering, but then he would not text for a while.

I had other playdates, so I was not simply waiting by the phone for him to be ready, but I would not pass on the opportunity to see what else we could explore with each other.

About a month after our time together, he texted me about how much he wanted to taste me again, he suggested when we could meet up, and I told him it would work for me. The next day, however, he said he would have to move the date. He had a "big project" that couldn't be moved. This was on a Sunday.

Whore Tip: Never ignore the red flags.

The third time he reached out, he finally suggested we have a picnic. He asked if I could take off in the middle of the day. Play hooky from work. The idea was fun and spontaneous, and I agreed. He told me he would text me the address and to bring my appetite. He also indicated that he had a surprise for me.

My imagination went wild. After the night I had suggested for us and how it turned out, I could not imagine what a "picnic" would hold in store.

That morning, he texted me the address. It looked like it was a small secluded park near a bridge halfway between our locations.

I decided on a cute sundress, flip flops, and a messy bun. This was a playful time of day and location, and I wanted to make the most of it.

As I pulled into the parking lot, the cute secluded picnic spot I had imagined began to melt away. This seemed to be a place for people to park who wanted to go fishing off the bridge.

There were several picnic tables resting nearby, not on grass but small rocks that made up the landscape. On the edge of the water were mangrove trees in clusters.

If you are not familiar with the mangrove tree, it is a tree that is found in the wetlands. It has vine-like roots that make it seem like they are out of a horror movie.

As I looked around, I found Ed sitting on a bench looking out at the water. I walked toward the table and saw there was a brown shopping bag atop it along with a small wrapped item.

"Hey gorgeous!" I said, trying to get his attention.

He turned, smiled, and stood up, meeting me partway. He took me in his arms, kissing me while spinning me around before he placed me down again.

"Are you hungry?" He led me back toward the table.

"Yes." I smiled and sat across from him.

There are moments in life when you realize what is handed to you is even better than what you expected. This was not one of those moments.

From the bag, he pulled out two grab-and-go lunches from a local grocery store and two bottled sodas.

I sat there wondering what in the hell was actually happening. It seemed like I had been thrust from a naughty adventure into a middle school lunch date.

He opened his lunch and began eating, gesturing for me to do the same. As I opened the package, I saw it contained half of a ham sandwich, some potato salad, and some diced fruit. I pulled out the spoon wrapped in a napkin and took a couple of bites.

We chatted about the drive and how the other's day had been. It was very casual conversation, and I was able to ask the name of his firm. He told me he was fifty percent owner with a friend from college. They were busy with projects, most of which were commercial buildings. I let him talk about his work as I tried to decide if this was really just a hiccup or more foreboding of things to come.

Whore Tip: Never ever ever ever ever ignore the red flags.

When he had finished his lunch completely and I had closed up mine, he slid the present over to me. From the size and feel, I could tell it was a book when I picked it up.

"I hope you like it. It reminded me of you," he said eagerly.

Unwrapping the book, I uncovered a book of love poems. Opening the cover and turning the pages, I found a handwritten dedication: "Thinking of you always, Ed."

"Wow," I said, nodding my head a little.

"I knew you would love it!" he said excitedly, moving to sit next to me.

I didn't love it or even like it. Actually, it was very weird.

He placed his hand on my thigh and moved it up toward my panties. He leaned in and kissed my neck, whispering in my ear, "Let's go into the trees."

"What?" The word escaped my lips before I could fully form what the hell I thought I should do next.

"Sneak into the trees with me, baby." He tried nuzzling my ear.

I stood up. "No."

He stood up as well, and I moved a couple steps back from him.

"I don't know what you think this is..." I gestured around us. "This is a place where fishermen grab their lunch.

And those..." I gestured at the trees. "...are a mangled mess where teenagers go to drink beer."

My voice held more than annoyance. "Did you think I would come down here and just fuck you in a bush after a cheap lunch?"

Before he responded, I interjected, "Don't answer that. I think if I knew your train of thought, it would just make it worse."

Putting the book down on the table, I walked away without turning around, even when he called my name.

Worst picnic ever!

As I drove home, I rolled the windows down and let the air rushing through the car take away some of the lingering disappointment.

Ed tried texting and calling several times. I ignored him.

One night while Alex was over watching a movie, I told her the whole story. When I got to the part where I said the name of his company, she googled it immediately. She found it...along with a picture of him and *his* family. As she looked deeper, she found that he was not in fact divorced. He was married with two children and his first name was not Ed; it was Mark.

I have said it before, and I will say it again: Married men are assholes!

20

BRINGING SEXY
BACK... AGAIN

After the Ed aka Mark situation, I kept to my known playmates for a while as finding a person to have sex with seemed like an easy prospect. The ones I had recently run across were proving to be landmines for me.

Even though several months had gone by, the situation with Jessie still stung when I thought about it. I knew that taking real dating off the table and only offering up sex, even really good sex, was not without the potential to have feelings creep in.

If you are around someone and talk to them for any time, it is easy to start caring about how they are doing. I am not talking about falling in love, but building a future is usually almost second nature to humans, even if that future was only for the next two hours.

> *Whore Tip: Make sure that line in the sand you draw never gets too blurry. It can be hard if you do not know when to cross back over.*

One of the most fun playmates I had when I originally started my adventures was Richard, or as I liked to call him, Brief Intermission.

At the time, he was nineteen to my thirty-two. I almost did not move forward with meeting him at first, but it was hard to turn down someone who looked almost exactly like Justin Timberlake.

Although I was not the first time having sex for him, I was someone who helped him build up his sexual prowess. When we would play, the experiences were all new to him. Wanting to master pleasing his partner was his goal, and I did not mind being practice.

We had explored each other for about eight months. In that time, he would come over almost every time I reached out, we would enjoy each other's company, and then he would leave.

The best part was that at no point did he become clingy. He understood the rules and abided by them perfectly.

I found it to be super cute the day he texted me that he had met someone and that we, of course, had to stop playing around. Although I missed the simplicity of what we shared, I knew that it was not going to be a forever situation. A part of me hoped that what we did together would help him in his relationships moving forward.

When I was curled up on the couch watching *Pitch Perfect* for the 1000th time and I got a text from him, I was pleasantly surprised.

Heya Gorgeous.

Hey BI. I should tell you that he found out that I called him Brief Intermission or BI to my friends. He thought it was funny, and this was another reason why what we did worked.

So... what are you up to this fine evening?

The only reason he would be texting me is if something, or more likely nothing, was happening with the new girl anymore.

This is the type of moment where I would be tempted to ask him what happened to her. I knew if I did, it would be a layer deeper than I wanted to go. I took a moment and then replied, *I was wondering if I should masturbate, or if I would find someone to help me out with it. Thoughts?*

BI at your service, Milady. How about an hour?

That works.

In case you are wondering, yes, it is a cheesy and perfectly fun interaction.

Whore Tip: Have fun, be playful, and remember that being silly is its own kind of therapy.

Although I would have loved to be cuddled on the couch when he arrived, I also wanted to be someone he wanted to touch, kiss, and lick. I needed a shower.

It took less than twenty minutes, and I was back in PJs on the couch with the door unlocked and condoms on the table.

Whore Tip: Always be prepared.

Almost to the minute, there was a knock on the door, and I told him to come inside.

The first thing I noticed was that his hair was shorter than the last time I saw him. He slid his shoes off and began unbuttoning his shirt.

I enjoyed simply watching as he peeled the clothes off his nicely defined frame.

"Whatcha watching?" He nodded in the direction of the TV.

"Thought that was obvious," I said, looking him up and down.

His smile widened, and he pounced on top of me.

I could smell his familiar cologne as he leaned in and kissed me, sending tingles through me as I kissed him deeper. My tongue found his as the pressure of him on top of me grew. Although I was still dressed and partially hidden by a blanket, his hard-on was unmistakable.

His hands framed my face as he pulled back for a moment, looking me in the eyes. "I missed this," he breathed and kissed me again.

Wrapping my arms around his shoulders, I ran my fingernails down his back. He thrust his tongue deeper into my mouth as if he could not get enough of my taste.

I moved to sit up, and he moved with me. I stood, casting the blanket to the side and pulling the PJ top over my head. I undid the tie holding the pants, so they fell to the floor. He started to stand, and I pushed him back to a sitting position so I could climb on top of him.

I leaned over, grabbed a condom off the table, and handed it to him. He smiled and slid it on.

Straddling his hips, it was easy to position his cock so I could slide down the shaft. Hands moved to cup my ass as I grabbed his shoulders. Rocking myself forward, I ground my clit against him as I rode him. A first, I took my time, riding all the way up, feeling his tip almost slide out and then back down again, feeling him stretch me the more aroused he became.

His hands moved from my ass to cup my breasts, then he used his fingers to tug on my erect nipples. The sound of my moans increased as I could feel climax growing closer. As I arched my back, he pushed my breasts together so he could suck on both my nipples at the same time.

This was all I needed to send me over the edge. Digging into his shoulder to hold on, I didn't want the sensation to stop.

His hands moved to my hips and held me in rhythm. This pressed my clit harder against him and I came again. With a final deep thrust, he jerked hard with his eruption, and it felt like my belly button was tingling.

Breathing deeply, we just held each other. My head rested on his shoulder, his fingers tracing small patterns across my back, causing me to tremble.

After a time, I rolled off his lap onto the couch, pulling the blanket up to cover myself. He removed the condom and went to the bathroom.

When he emerged, he dressed again, then leaned in to kiss my cheek.

"You know how to make a guy feel amazing." His voice was almost a whisper.

I looked up at him and winked. "I think that is a trait we both share, Handsome."

He held my gaze for a moment longer and then left, closing the door behind him.

I got up, grabbing my PJs, and headed toward the bathroom locking the front door on my way by. I couldn't help but wonder what void I had just filled for him.

> *Whore Tip: Sometimes you will be exactly what that person needs in that moment, and sometimes, they will return the favor.*

21

Sink or Swim

Archer called, said he wanted to go out dancing, and I should get ready. Since it was almost nine at night, I had no plans and was sitting on the couch with a good book and a pint of ice cream. I almost replied no.

Then I re-read the text. It wasn't a question. I knew Archer was probably already on his way over to "do my hair" for tonight.

A perk of having a friend who is a hairdresser is that, if you are going out, you will be dressed to impress. Well, at least your hair will be. Bonus if they have any fashion sense because they will not let you out of the house without a complimenting outfit.

> *Whore Tip: If you are going to put effort in, go all the way. You never get a second chance to make a first impression.*

I was correct in my assumption that he was on his way. As I was stepping out of the shower, there was a knock on the door. I answered with my towel on, and he gave me two air kisses on the cheeks, ordered me to hurry, and took up residence on the couch.

I headed to the bedroom and started to decide what to wear, but then realized I had no idea where we were going.

"What club are we going to?"

"Freaky-Tiki," he replied.

"Where?" I didn't know the place.

"Freaky-Tiki," he stated again. One of my pet peeves in life is when you ask a question to get clarification and the person simply repeats what they said to begin with. Super annoying.

"What is Freaky-Tiki?"

"It is a bar up on 19."

Highway 19 ran the length of the county and mostly contained car dealers and fast-food locations. It took me a moment of racking my brain before it dawned on me.

"You don't mean that weird bar in the shopping center with the hot-dog themed restaurant?"

"That is the one."

I stuck my head into the living room.

"You're kidding, right? That place looks..." I couldn't think of the right word.

"Dirty," he said without looking away from whatever he had put on the TV. "You meant to say dirty, and yes, that is the one, so hurry up."

I ended up spending a lot less time trying to impress and threw on some skinny jeans and a cute but casual shirt. I also chose a pair of cute sneakers. I was not going to put my feet down on those floors.

Finishing off my look with simple but sexy make-up, I let Archer work his magic on my hair.

We took an Uber to the Freaky-Tiki, and when we got out, it was exactly everything I thought it would be.

It was on the corner of a strip mall, the opposite end from the hot-dog restaurant I mentioned and then a few other places, including a pawn shop.

The bar/club had built a small deck along the side adorned with palm leaves and unlit tiki torches strapped to the railing. Besides offering full ambiance, this also seemed to function as the smoking area.

"This seems like a terrible idea," I told Archer, knowing I was not going to change his mind no matter what I said.

"It is." He nodded, and we headed to the door.

There was a line to the entrance, which in a way surprised me, and once we got past the hulking gatekeepers, aka bouncers, I understood why.

When we entered, the scantily clad hostess asked us if we wanted the $10 or $20 option. I was not sure what she was talking about, and before I could ask her, Archer handed her $40, and she handed us two blue solo cups.

I took mine and followed him to the packed bar.

After securing our place in line to ask for a drink, I looked around. The club was laid out to have a large dance floor, two bars, a small section of tables, and a couple of pool tables in the back.

As I scanned the crowd, I saw a mixture of tourists, college aged kids, people our age, and even a couple guys playing pool who looked like they were in a biker gang. What did we all have in common? Red or blue cups.

Sink or Swim is when you pay a flat amount and can drink as much as you want. Red cups meant well drinks, blue name brand. As Archer handed me back my first Jack and Coke, the certainty that this was a terrible idea sank in.

> *Whore Tip: Trust yourself more than you trust any-*
> *thing else. About both trivial things and big things.*
> *You are your number one champion.*

After taking a few sips, we walked out onto the dance floor. The music ended up being a stream of dance and party favorites. Although many clubs want to be on the cutting edge of what is new in the music world, this one seemed to know its place. People came here to drink and party, and that is exactly what was offered.

By the sixth or seventh refill, Archer ended up sitting at one of the tables drunk-texting his girlfriend while I continued to dance.

I danced and drank, and that little voice in my head was screaming I was way beyond buzzed or tipsy and into the territory where I made bad choices. I ignored it and went to refill my cup.

Handing my cup to the bartender, I heard someone say, "You are fucking hot" in my ear. I turned to see a guy about my height, slim, with a crooked smile and spiked white hair.

Although there were flashing lights from the dance floor, the room was a little too dark or I was a little too drunk for details.

"Thanks," I said, grinning.

"What's your name?" He leaned in close to my ear so I could hear him over the music.

"Randi."

"Spike," he said back.

I don't think his name was actually Spike. I think it might have been Mike or Brad or who the hell knows. My drunk brain at the time went with Spike.

"Cool," I replied just as the bartender handed me my drink.

"Cheers!" I held my cup aloft, and we clinked our cups together as much as plastic could clink.

I turned and made my way back to the dance floor. He followed me.

Swaying my hips to whatever Ke$ha song was playing, I let him move in to dance with me. Placing his hand on my hips, he pulled our bodies together. Moving with the sounds of the bass, I could feel the heat between us.

He grabbed my hand, spun me out, then pulled me back to him. His hand went around my waist. I could feel his fingers holding on while his hard-on pushed against me through his pants.

I got a chill as his lips touched my neck.

As he continued to nibble and play, my desire grew with tingles spreading from my core.

His fingers began to play with the waist of my jeans and...

"We're leaving." Archer grabbed my arm.

It took me a second to shake the fog.

"What?" I asked.

He grabbed the drink from my hand, putting it on the table as he moved me toward the door of the club.

"Dude, what the fuck?" This was from Spike following us and holding on to my other arm.

Archer stopped and turned looking at Spike.

"I'm sorry. My girlfriend gets a little too flirty when she is drunk," he told him. Spike let go of my arm.

"Girlfriend?" My face was a mask of confusion.

"Yep, Sweetness. We should go." Archer's voice was insistent.

"Your girlfriend is here?" I obviously wasn't catching the hint.

"He's not your boyfriend?" Spike asked.

"No." I shook my head.

"Yes," insisted Archer.

Spike grabbed my hand and wrote something on it. Before I could say anything more, a car honked its horn, and I found myself in the backseat.

"I'm hungry," I said as we started to drive.

My head was spinning a little bit, and I looked down at my hand to see what Spike had written. It was a number. I pulled out my phone and typed it in as Archer was discussing something with the driver.

Let the drunk-texting begin:

Me: *Hey*

Spike: *Who's that dude?*

Me: *Archr*

Spike: *Boyfriend?*

Me: *Nope*

Spike: *Ur so fucking hot*

Me: *You 2*

Spike: *I want ur pussy*

Me: *So Hot*

Spike: *Come back*

"Spike said for me to come back," I tell Archer
"Oh my god. Give me your phone." Archer reached for my phone.
"No!" I tried to hold on to it.
"Give. Me. The. Phone," he said really loudly.
 I handed him the phone.
There is a part of my drunk self that knows I should listen to my friends.

> *Whore Tip: Pick friends that have your back always.*
> *Then trust them always.*

The car began to slow, and I unclicked my seatbelt.
"We're not home. How many cheeseburgers do you want?"
"Cheeseburgers?"
"How many?"
"Ten."
I tried to reattach my seatbelt and found it too hard so I gave up, laying my head back, then the world went dark.

22

CHEESEBURGERS
IN PARADISE

I am sure you have guessed that I SANK.

Whore Tip: Sink or Swim is basically a bar or club equivalent of self-hazing. There is no way possible to end up swimming or even treading water. Avoid it at all costs.

I woke in the morning in my bed, well, on my bed. I was still dressed, including my shoes. As I started to peel myself off the bed, the first thing that came into focus was a cheeseburger, still kind of in its wrapper with two chunks eaten out of it.

There were two more cheeseburgers on the floor with a couple bites out of them.

I felt terrible.

Moving very slowly, I sat on the end of the bed and removed my sneakers and socks. The room was spinning.

I walked, actually I stumbled, down the hallway toward the bathroom. There was a still wrapped cheeseburger resting in the sink.

After peeing and debating a shower, I made my way back toward the living room. I found Archer asleep on the couch with a fast-food bag and several wrappers on the table next to my phone.

Finding that it was out of charge, I plugged it in and started brewing some coffee. Realizing how long each of these actions took me, I concluded that I was still drunk.

Some people don't realize and have fortunately never experienced being so drunk that even hours of sleep do not remove enough alcohol from your system to sober up. This was me.

I decided the shower was needed.

Grabbing some PJs because I wasn't getting dressed in real clothes anytime soon, I made my way to take a shower.

The hot water felt amazing and I took my time. Any sudden movements caused either dizziness or nausea, but I managed to clean the night off of myself.

Drying off, I noticed there was writing on my hand. It was mostly faded, but it looked like numbers. I stared at it trying to make out the numbers as I brushed my teeth (after having thrown the cheeseburger in the sink away).

After dressing, I poured some coffee for the both of us. I heard Archer starting to stir. When I opened the cabinet to grab cups, I found a cheeseburger still in a wrapper.

I threw it away and poured the coffee.

Grabbing some cream out of the fridge, I found two, wait, three more of the burgers. Still in wrappers. I left them there.

As I sat on the couch, I handed Archer his cup.

"So drunk," he said before taking a sip.

The coffee tasted more amazing than usual.

Breaking the silence, I said, "I do not remember what happened after..." I tried to think of the exact last moment I remembered.

I hated being that drunk.

Whore Tip: Black-out drunk does not look sexy on anyone. Literally anyone.

"Okay, I remember dancing and you sitting at the table." I hoped that was close to the departure time.

Archer smirked. "Do you remember Spike?"

"Spike?" I looked down at my hand and the writing on it. It said Mike.

Before he could say anything else, I grabbed my phone out of the bedroom and looked at my text messages. This Mike/Spike person had texted me about fifteen more times last night and this morning.

"Please tell me I did not do anything too stupid," I muttered to myself as I walked back in and sat on the couch.

"I intervened before anything to crazy happened."

"Was he at least hot?"

"See for yourself!" Archer handed me his phone with a picture displayed of me drunk smiling, with a man, slightly taller than me, most likely a decade or so older than me but dressed in skater clothes who had badly bleached hair, pock-marked skin, and a missing tooth in the front. He looked like what would happen if you did a "where are they now?" with a nineties boy band.

Handing the phone back, I went to get the coffee.

Spike, as Archer refers to him, texted me for several months even though I never replied. I even ran into him twice at bars. Once I was able to hide so he couldn't see me, and the second time I pretended that I did not recognize him. This generated more texts and two calls.

Saying that was the worst part of the experience would have been easy if I had not found cheeseburgers all over my house for the next couple of weeks. It is actually scary how well-preserved fast food can be—unlike my dignity at times.

23

THE PROPOSITION

O n the dating apps where I did some of my hunting for play-mates, I would often receive requests from remarkably interesting people.

I try not to judge a person's sexual appetites as long as they do not hurt another person or creature. Having gotten requests to be a dominatrix which included putting that particular man's junk in a dick cage (I suggest you Google this, at work of course) all the way to a friendly wolf-furry asking me to be a fox with him (again, you should Google the term), I was rarely surprised when approached online.

That was, of course, until Albert.

Albert sent me a message one night that said he thought I was beautiful. He liked what my profile said and had an interesting proposition for me that involved multiple partners, but I would be the only woman involved. Would I be interested in hearing it?

Normally I would have just ignored this type of message, but I must say I was intrigued.

Further scanning his profile, I learned that Albert was a rather good-looking gentleman in his late fifties. He worked as a pilot for a major shipping company and flew around the country regularly and enjoyed tasty food, good wine, and traveling. Of course, most of this profile was pretty standard.

I reached out with simple *Tell me more.*

He was quick to reply, telling me that he was a couple of years from retiring, he wanted to travel the world, and was looking for a person to do that with. This seemed pretty normal.

The not as normal part was that he wanted a woman who was willing to have sex with other men.

Now, I had encountered this previously with a man I called Red Sox on Whore Island. Erik was his real name. He was a huge baseball fan; the nickname fit.

Red Sox wanted to have a girlfriend who was willing to sleep with other guys. Not in his presence, of course, but the girlfriend was supposed to immediately come and have sex with him afterward. During the sex, he wanted his girlfriend to tell him all about the encounter she had just had—every detail. That was his kink.

> *Whore Tip: Never judge a kink. It doesn't have to be something that you participate in, but don't shame what gets another person off.*

This, at the time, was not something I was interested in. I also found out that I was not extremely interested in Erik either. It worked itself out.

Albert wanted to meet over a glass of wine to discuss his desires.

It might have been overwhelming curiosity or wondering if I had a kink that had not been ignited yet, but I knew I had to hear this out.

I discussed Albert with Alex, and she thought that it was most likely not going to be something I was into; however, she insisted that I call her right after with full details. She also insisted on the nickname: Benedick.

When I asked her why, she told me that it was a character in the play *Much Ado About Nothing*, a character who rails against marriage but then gets married because he is talked into it by his friends.

I told her I thought it was very cultured of her, and she told me to fuck off. She lost some culture points there.

We decided to meet a few days later at a wine bar that I suggested. It was a cute little place in a part of town I did not frequent often in case Benedick was not what he appeared; I did not have the chance of running into him like I had with Spike.

It was in the middle of Florida summer so dressing in anything that was not comfortable, even if mostly inside, wouldn't work. I chose a sundress, light make-up, and hair in a tight ponytail.

As I entered, I found he had already gotten us a table with a cheese plate. He stood and greeted me with a warm hug and a kiss on the cheek. He pulled out my chair to one of the few high-top tables.

He handed me the wine list and asked what I was in the mood for. I perused the list and chose a Malbec that I had the last time I was had been here. When the waitress came over, he ordered us a bottle.

Although I would not have said Albert was my type, he was attractive for his age. He was well built, had a dark tan, and I could tell he dyed his hair to maintain the deep brown color I was sure he had in his youth.

The one feature that stood out more than any other was his dazzling smile. He had aged very well.

When the bottle was brought to the table, he toasted, "To possibilities." I toasted back, taking a drink, and waited for the explanation of the proposition.

Benedick told me that he had just recently ended the type of relationship he was going to ask me about. He had been with his last girlfriend for three years, but when she had finished her master's degree, she decided they were no longer a fit.

This told me that he liked them younger, which is not a terrible thing, just helps to understand the fantasy.

He wanted to have a woman in his life that he could care for completely.

What did this mean? He was willing and able to have her be a kept woman. He didn't want her to work because this would get in the way of travelling.

This sounded sweet, I supposed, but it was just the beginning.

He was a member of an exclusive sex club and expected his companion to participate with him.

I asked what exactly an "exclusive sex club" was. I imagined it was something like the movie *Eyes Wide Shut* with Mr. Cruise. Having friends that were also part of swinger's clubs and groups where you could swap your partners, I knew sex clubs were genuinely a thing. I had just never gone to one, even though I had been invited.

"How would you feel about having sex while a group of people watched?"

"I don't know. Would you be picking the partner or would I?"

His companion, he kept calling it that, apparently, could choose whom she slept with. However, he wanted to be part of the interaction.

"Part of the interaction?"

"If I want him to fuck her harder, for instance, or in a different position, then I give instructions."

"What if she doesn't acquiesce to your request?" I threw in a little pirate speak.

"I would hope that I would never ask something that she wouldn't want to do."

I knew from the look in his eyes any partner would have to want to do what he wished. There was not going to be a lot of telling him no.

"Are you sleeping with others as well?" I asked.

"No. I only have sex with her. I am monogamous."

"I do not think that is the right word to describe this situation."

He smiled. "You are clever."

"So, the companion, she chooses from other members of this sex club?"

"No."

He was still trying to gauge my interest.

"How long have you been in relationships like this?"

"Over a decade."

"How many relationships like this?"

"Four."

I paused, taking a sip of wine, or three, debating how far down this rabbit hole I wanted to go.

"How many members are part of the sex club?"

"There are several couples, about twenty."

"All couples?"

"You always have to bring a partner."

He leaned in closer as he spoke.

"Are you interested?"

I chose not to answer that direct of a question and made him finish laying out all the details.

"Do the men always watch?"

"Yes.

Is having your partner watch a fantasy of yours, Randi?"

"It hasn't been one, no."

> *Whore Tip: Be willing to explore new options but only to the extent you feel safe. You can, of course, be nervous, but you should never feel terrible about your actions.*

"So, you have never wanted someone to watch?"

He rubbed the tip of his finger up and down the stem of his wine glass.

"I have never wanted a third party to watch me and a partner," I said honestly. "However, I have chosen to have sex in places where that could have been possible, but not as an intended consequence."

"I am wondering what you think so far of my proposition?"

I picked up another piece of cheese and took a moment to assess. Although what he was saying wasn't the weirdest thing I had ever heard—dick cage, for instance, which I had to Google—I did not know exactly how I felt about what he was asking me.

"I am still processing." I paused. "

You mentioned the men only watch." I moved on to the next logical question. "Who are the woman sleeping with then?"

"The club will vet men in their early to mid-twenties who meet with the qualifications."

"Is protection used?"

"Sometimes. If the woman, her partner, or the man are willing to not use it, then sometimes they don't." His slight shrug and the tone of his voice told me he had made this choice before. My first instinct was that this was unsafe. I, however, have not always made the best choices, and I wasn't in the position of actually having sex right now. So as the lawyers say, the point was moot.

"Do you like to have sex with strangers?" he asked.

"I have had sex with people I have just met and enjoyed it."

"So, this idea would not be new." He seemed to check some box in his mind.

"It is in the aspect of walking into a location specifically to fuck a person there. I do not think what I have done is exactly that."

He smiled. "I think you have if you, for instance, had sex right after meeting someone." I could tell this statement, he thought, had proven his point.

"Although I am willing to have sex with someone I don't 'know,' I usually choose to move forward. I am not arriving with the intent already established. I am also not letting someone else choose things for me. This changes the dynamics."

He leaned back a little, taking a sip of his wine.

I knew for certain, without having to weigh any other parts of this situation, that Benedick wanted to be in complete control of his partner. Not in a submissive sort of way, but he wanted to be the "man" and wanted to his companion to want what he wanted for her. This was not going to be something I ever wanted as a type of relationship.

"What else do you want to know?" He hadn't given up that he might tempt me back in.

"How are the men chosen?"

"If any members of the club see someone they find interesting, then they proposition them. If the person is interested, then they vet them to make sure they will be a good fit. Some of the time it is word of mouth from one of the men to friends. The same process is done."

"Members? Both male and female?"

"The men mostly."

I was not surprised.

"How do you decide if they are a good fit?"

"We look for certain qualities."

"Qualities, huh? Such as?"

He took the slow last sip of the wine in his glass.

"Randi," his voice sounded huskier, "before I reveal all my secrets, does this idea or do I interest you?"

I took my time drinking the last bit of wine in my glass.

"Be..Albert," my voice was sultry, "I haven't decided yet."

A grin spread across his face "Why don't you sleep on it?"

"Good idea," I agreed.

He paid the check as I ordered an Uber. He offered to walk me to the location where it would be arriving.

"Well, this was a very interesting night," I said as we got to the spot.

"Yes, it was," he said as he leaned in, quickly kissing me.

Having not expected the kiss, I was not the best at reciprocating it. His lips were almost as forceful as his tongue, which might have been nice if I was prepared.

As he pulled back, he said, "I wanted you to have a taste what you were in for."

I was happy to get the notification when the car arrived.

"Loads to think about," I said as I got in and closed the door.

Whore Tip: Even if you may be interested in something at first, you have every right to abandon ship whenever you want to.

24

THE FINE PRINT

I called Alex on the way home and tried to replay the entire conversation to her. As I explained points, I was impressed with how patient she was with every detail I tried to fill in.

I finished and she asked the main question I had that did not get answered.

"What kind of guys?"

Since I did not know, and Benedick thought I was thinking about my interest, I would ask him for clarification tomorrow.

We talked some more about what it would mean to be in this type of relationship. This was not something she or I would actually consider. Neither of us was the type to let the man make most of the choices.

Some might be mad at my thought process on this, but I feel if that is something a person enjoys and prefers, then that is their choice.

Alex made me promise to tell her when and if he told me the titillating news on the men. When I hung up the phone, it occurred to me that my driver had heard the whole conversation. I was not embarrassed, but I also felt like realizing this caused a silence to hang in the air.

"It doesn't have to be weird," the driver said.

I looked up. We were parked at a light, and he was turned so I could see the side of his face. He was handsome. Well, the half of his face I could see was handsome.

"What if I was hoping it would be weird?" I winked.

He smiled as the light turned green and he put his attention back on the road. "I suppose if you wanted to make it weird, you would tell me you had a fantasy of having sex with a hot Lyft driver while your Uber driver watched."

This made me laugh.

> *Whore Tip: A perfect moment can be summed up in a good laugh. Treasure it.*

"Well..." I looked at my phone for his name, "Jordan. I am not sure how you guessed my kink. But with your five-star rating, I hope you're willing to do what it takes to keep it."

This time he laughed as we pulled onto my street. He pulled up to the end of my driveway, put the car in park, and turned so I could see his entire face.

His skin was almost a bronzed chestnut color, and his hair was dark and cut close. He had a strong jaw, defined cheekbones, and perfectly kissable lips surrounding a very sexy smile.

"What if I changed my mind about which driver gets to watch?" I asked playfully.

He let his smile morph into a sultrier look, and he said, "I think you might be as smart as you are beautiful."

I laughed again and so did he. He was playful and I enjoyed him.

"Thank you for the ride, Jordan," I said as I opened the door, and the light came on, revealing his deep amber-colored eyes. "Any chance you might be willing to give me a ride in the future?"

"It would be my pleasure," he said and reached in his glove compartment and handed me a card.

I took the card and got out of the car.

He waited until I got inside the house before pulling away.

All in all, not a bad night, I thought as I got ready for bed.

After a good night's sleep and some more time to think on it, I knew that although he left me in mystery, I did not actually care what kind of men were involved in the sex club. I wasn't interested at all, based on the guidelines he explained, so no point in following the rabbit down the hole further.

That was of course until I checked my messages on my phone and saw the text Benedick had sent: *A little taste of what you could be in for.* It was five photos of men, all of them humongous, like obscene bodybuilder sized in the body, and huge cocks.

The men of the sex couple wanted to have their women dominated in bed, in almost every way it seemed.

I forwarded the message and the photos to Alex, and within moments received her reply: *Oh Dear God!*

Taking a long hot shower, I found my thoughts drifting to Jordan and wondering what he was packing under all those clothes. My fingers drifted as well thinking of how those lips of his would feel on any part of me.

After getting dressed, I decided to text Benedick and let him know that although I appreciated the time he spent with me, I was not interested in what he was offering.

He asked if I was sure, and when I said that I was, he wished me luck.

With that done, I texted Jordan: *Wanna make it weird?*

He texted back a brief time later: *Do I need to invite a Lyft driver?*

This was going to be fun!

25

LOL

So, this comic and a redhead walk into a bar...
We were sitting in our favorite people watching spot, the café at the local bookstore, and Baley decided that what we needed to do was shake things up a bit.

She had won tickets to a local comedy club and wanted us all to go.

One thing that maybe some do not know is that comedy clubs give out a ton of tickets. Why? Because you are required to buy at least two drinks with said ticket, and the drinks are never reasonably priced.

Of course, you may get two to three hours of enjoyment, and with any luck, you will laugh your ass off. The two drinks, which I am sure make things potentially funnier, are worth it.

Sally said she would drive since she wasn't drinking, which was fantastic.

Due to it being a "girls' night," it was only when we arrived that Alex ask who we were seeing.

Looking at the signage, it was no one we had ever heard of. Also, you usually have one or two opening acts before the headliner, who in this case was a female comic.

The venue, located in a strip mall in Tampa, had a small lobby with only a few chairs and a couch, and of course a bar.

We decided to start the evening with a drink. We had stopped for dinner on the way. As we ordered, the person behind the bar was quick to point out that any drinks purchased in the lobby did not count toward the two-drink minimum, and we needed to keep this in mind. Of course, this was after he poured the drinks and put them on the bar.

Looking over at Alex, I could tell she was gearing up to say something. Instead, as I was about to jump in, a guy stepped up and said, "Put them on my tab, Mike."

"You didn't have to do that," I said, turning to look at our benefactor.

It was his royal blue eyes that grabbed me at first.

"You're welcome," he said, smiling and tipping his glass in my direction.

Tipping mine back, I said, "I'm Randi. This is Sally, Baley, and Alex," introducing the girls in order. He shook hands with each of them. "Nice to meet all of you. I'm Dave.

Is this your first time?"

"To this club? Yes. How about yourself?" Baley asked.

He grinned as the bartender snorted. "I have been here a few times."

Before he could clarify, the door opened on the back wall, and it was announced that we should find our seats.

"See you soon," he winked.

Smiling, I replied, "I hope so." We headed inside.

We had barely sat down before Sally said, "He was nice."

"Nice?" quipped Baley. "He was hot."

Alex nodded. "His hair was amazing. I'm a little jealous, not going to lie."

His hair had been a dark brown that was long and thick.

The waitress came by, and we placed another drink order along with some appetizers.

"He had the kind of hair you could hold on to," I said, trying to sound casual.

Baley nearly spit out her drink. "Randi!"

"What? It is true. Did you see his eyes? I would love to see those staring down or up at me, if you know what I mean." I did a head tilt which caused Baley and Sally to giggle.

"I think we all know what you mean," Alex said, teasing.

Whore Tip: Take time to genuinely enjoy your friends. Those are memories you get to hold onto.

The waitress brought our drinks and the lights dimmed.

The host came on stage and welcomed everyone with a few jokes, then introduced the first comic of the night. It was a guy named Chris something. He was funny, the jokes mostly about being a truck driver.

Then he announced the next act: Dave. When he walked under the spotlight, I was able to truly drink him all in.

Even in the jeans and button-down, I could tell he was tall and slender; he had a well-trimmed beard that went with the long hair.

He grabbed the mic. "Hello, I am Dave."

The audience responded, "Hi Dave."

"I was going to come out with a fantastic joke about what it is like to bang a soulless ginger I once dated, but I met a super-hot redhead in the lobby, and since I am hoping to get her number later, I decided to shelve it. Although now that I have said that out loud, I most likely have just friend-zoned myself."

Most of the audience laughed and a few called out things like "You're screwed dude!" and "How hot was she?" Everyone at my table, however, was laughing and teasing me. A few people at the tables immediately around us looked over.

I think I might have even blushed a little. Not out of embarrassment. He thought I was hot enough to bring me up in his set. But this was the most public way I had ever been hit on.

Since the spotlight was so bright, I was sure that anyone on stage looking out at the audience wouldn't be able to see beyond the front row.

He continued his set and was super funny.

Comedy is, of course, about being funny, but a huge part of it is timing. His was pretty amazing.

When he finished, the host came out and introduced the headliner: Krystyna Hutchinson. It turned out that she was actually a co-host to a podcast called *Guys We Fucked*.

She was hysterical and real, joking about men and one-night stands. She had us rolling the whole time. All of us girls ended up listening to the podcast after and loved it.

Whore Tip: Listen to Guys We Fucked (the podcast)!

After the show, we got up and headed to the lobby, and I saw Dave standing at the bar. He walked over toward us. He addressed the girls,

"Do you mind if I borrow Randi for a moment?"

"Not at all," Alex replied, winking at me. "We'll meet you at the car."

We walked over to the bar as everyone was encouraged to leave; they were getting ready for the next audience.

You will find that you do not get to loiter in these places.

"What did you think?" he asked.

I scrunched my face a little. "You know it is super cheesy when you ask a girl that, right?"

He laughed.

"My apologies" he said. "I just wanted to know if that was too much."

"Which part?" I teased. "The part where you mentioned me on stage? Or the part where you were wondering what I looked like with my top off?"

I don't think he was expecting the bluntness with how wide his eyes went.

"Wow... You're..."

"Blunt? Funny? Hot?" I was not holding back.

"Yes to all of that." His smile was playful, but his eyes looked hungry.

"Then why haven't you given me your number yet?"

He grabbed his phone and opened it, handing it to me. I typed in my number, and as the name, I put Hot Red Head. Handing the phone back, I said, "It has been very pleasurable meeting you, Dave." I did a little look up and down him with my eyes and turned to head out.

Sometimes you just have to make an exit.

I got in the car; the girls wanted details, so of course I shared what happened.

"Your milkshake really does bring all the boys to the yard!" Sally laughed. "I only seem to get them to the property line."

"Your hubby would kill them if they made it to the house," Alex chimed in, "so maybe that is for the best."

Not long after we headed home, I got a text from Dave: *You really know how to work a room. Consider me captivated.*

You have no idea, I replied, adding him as The Comedian in my phone.

> *Whore Tip: Never be afraid to make an impression other than showing the real you. You only want people who appreciate you in your life.*

26

COMEDY OF CONDOMS

I decided to meet with The Comedian after a few days of texting. To say he was eager was an understatement. Although he did shows a couple of nights a week and also had "practice sessions" once a week as well, he wanted to make time for me. I took it as a compliment.

We decided to get together on a Wednesday night. He invited me to his condo. I told Sally and followed all the normal rules for safety.

It turned out that he lived about ten minutes from my house, so he fell into the very convenient category if this ended up being something I wanted to repeat.

He lived on bottom floor of the building. I raised my hand to knock, but he opened the door before my knuckles made contact.

"You're here," he said.

"Did you think I would not show?" I teased as I walked inside. "I mean, to be honest, I debated it, but I figured that there was nothing on TV tonight."

"Well, you could have checked Netflix," he said.

I smirked and headed back towards the door. "Crap, you're right... I am sure I could find something to binge."

As I got near the door, he closed the distance between us, spinning me around and pushing me against the door as it closed.

When his lips met mine, he ravaged them. The pressure was strong, and his hand moved up to the back of my neck. His tongue slid in deep, tasting me. His desire was unbridled.

Finally pulling back, he breathed, "God, I have wanted to do that since the moment I saw you."

He leaned in again before I could reply and began kissing me again. The warmth of his lips sent tingles down my spine. I could almost taste how much he wanted me.

I reached up to undo the buttons on his shirt, and he froze for a second. I almost stopped, but then he pulled up my shirt and the only break between our contact was to pull it over my head.

He looked as if he was going to say something, but I brought my lips to his again.

There was so much fire I didn't want it to stop. I was craving contact with all of him. I couldn't pull our clothes off fast enough.

His hands caressed my skin, and heat trails followed his touch. This was the feeling I wanted in a playmate.

Whore Tip: Do not overthink it!!

It wasn't long before all of our clothes were on the floor, and we were moving to the bedroom. His eyes roamed all over me, drinking me in.

The room was lit by only a small lamp, and the bed was unmade. This told me he wasn't counting on this happening. That made it even more alluring.

Moving onto the bed, he laid on his side with one knee bent. I could tell he made room for me to slide in beside him.

I drank him in, his long hair falling on his shoulders, his very fit body, and his massive hard cock. My eyes widened and my breath quickened.

I had not seen a cock nearly that size since Jared (see *Whore Island*) and that one had been hard to take, no pun intended.

I could tell that Dave's muscles tensed when my eyes beheld his thick shaft. His eyes met mine, and there was a little apprehension. I had seen a look similar to this before with Jared. His cock had been so large that women had flat out turned him down for that reason. Unfortunately, after our first time, I had to tell him that I could not have him penetrate me again. He was heartbroken.

I looked into Dave's eyes and smiled, sliding into bed next to him. The relief showed in his features. There were some things I knew we would not be able to do, such as anal, and I knew I would have to have some time in between our encounters, but if he was as amazing at fucking me as he was at kissing me, then I would deal with any soreness.

He leaned in, nuzzling my neck, planting light kisses from the nape of my neck to my earlobe. The tip of his tongue traced the line of my jaw to my lips until he took my mouth to his again, and he laid me down on my back.

Warmth pooled between my legs as he moved my arms above my head and licked from my lips to between my breasts. He moved to kneel between my legs, spreading them apart.

It was his turn to explore me with his eyes. There was anticipation in his gaze, and I moaned as he used his fingertips to trace from my neckline down my chest and stomach to the peak of my wetness.

Fingertips caressed the skin between my thighs and my center. The softness of his tongue touched mixed with the heat of his skin sent me over the edge. I climaxed, closing my eyes and trying to hold myself in place as not to lose the sensation.

Just as I felt it begin to subside, his fingers penetrated me, and he bent down, taking my now erect nipple into his mouth. Sucking on me harder sent me into rapture all over again. Adding a finger as my walls contracted around him, he was testing how much I could take.

I wanted more.

He moved to the other nipple, ensuring both had equal pleasure. His teeth grazed me as his tongue flicked against my tip, and the ecstasy rolled over me, my eyes fluttering, unable to hold them open. I was in bliss.

The air hitting my nipple when his mouth pulled back sent shivers down my entire body. I heard the noise of a drawer opening and the sound of a condom being ripped open.

I opened my eyes to watch him sheath his length.

I wrapped one leg around him, encouraging him not to hesitate. I did not want to lose this feeling.

Holding his length, he guided it inside, entering me slowly. I moved my hips to meet his movements, then looked him in the eyes. "Now."

That was all the encouragement he needed, and he thrust himself inside of me, putting his hands down next to my shoulders.

He used his hips and thighs to keep me slightly elevated to the angle was just what he needed. As he thrust harder, I ran my hands up his arms to his shoulders and wrapped my legs around him to get my own leverage, meeting every one of his thrusts.

His cock filled my entire sleeve, hitting my cervix. Although there was slight pain, I simply arched my back a little more, then we found the rhythm.

I erupted again and tightened my walls around his thickness. Through the wetness, I could feel him pulsing, and opening my eyes to meet his, I knew he was close.

With his next thrust, I growled, "Cum in my pussy!"

One final deep thrust, and he came hard. Arching his back, his fingers dug into the sheets, holding me in place.

Pure rapture.

Whore Tip: Relish those perfect moments of pleasure.

After a moment, he laid down on top of me, trying to catch his breath. His face so close to mine. We laid together for a time. My entire body felt electrified; every touch was sensitive. I was grateful for the time to come down from this level of stimulation. I knew that I would want to reach it again. I hoped The Comedian could be added to the roster on a regular basis.

27

HAUNTED BY THE PAST

I left his condo as soon as my legs would hold me. He asked me to stay the night, but although we had chatted about what I was looking for, I needed to make sure that he was, in fact, able to follow the rules.

I pulled into my driveway and texted Sally, letting her know I was safe and sound. Happy to hear that I did not in fact need a SWAT team called, she told me that she wanted all the details at dinner with the girls, which we had scheduled for Thursday night.

I told her I would see her then.

There was still a nice smile on my face as I walked up to my door. In the middle of the doormat was a huge vase full of lavender and white roses.

I looked around to see if I had missed an unfamiliar car on my street. It was late and the hairs on the back of my neck stood up.

I picked up the vase and went inside, closing the door and setting it on the dining room table.

Stepping back from the arrangement, I took a deep breath, got a cold glass of water, and took a few more breaths.

Whore Tip: Trust your gut. If something throws you off, you need to make sure you take the time you need

*to approach the situation. Don't force yourself if you
are not ready.*

There were at least two if not three dozen roses in the vase. They
were a mixture of lavender with white coloration of the roses. They
were called goddess roses. I knew this because in my last relationship, the one that ended when he cheated on me, we had discussed
getting married.

I closed my eyes, doing some deep yoga breaths. You count to
four in and out, if you were wondering.

Why did this bother me so much? He had been gone for over a
year. I was in a much better place than even the last time I had seen
him, which was when he had shown up at my house to show me a
new suit he bought and tell me how this proved he had changed.

Lucky for me, the girls had been there, and more importantly,
Alex was having none of it.

That was the last time I had heard anything.

You may not believe me, but I didn't even social media stalk him.

*Whore Tip: Let your past be the past. It doesn't matter
what your ex is doing. There is a reason they are an
ex: keep it that way.*

Part of me wanted to sleep on this. I had a fucking amazing
night, and it was deflated the moment I saw the flowers.

It is interesting how the universe works. I could have stayed with
The Comedian and then what would have happened to the flowers
overnight? Would they have been knocked over? Vase shattered
and glass everywhere?

I should just throw them away.

Fuck!

Part of me wanted to call Alex. I knew calling Sally or Baley
would possibly end with trying to comfort me, and I did not

want comfort. I needed to not feel like this when something small happened.

I was pacing.

This was stupid.

It was just flowers.

"Get it together, Randi!"

Yes, I was talking to myself, and yes, I needed to take some of my own advice. If a friend called me and told me that they were going through exactly what I was, I would tell them to read the damn card or throw the flowers away.

> *Whore Tip: A trigger is just that. When you encounter one, take your own advice.*

Nodding, I walked up to the table, pulled the card off the flowers, and opened it.

The nights are so lonely without my Goddess
                    -   Your Watusi
                    -

What in the actual fuck?

Dropping the card on the table, I felt my anxiety shift into anger. Jessie.

I continued pacing. I knew that these were not delivered; he had brought them. This meant he could be outside right now. Jessie had been a mercenary-for-hire for years. I would not have seen him outside unless he wanted me to.

How did he know about the flowers? Had I told him about them at some point? Did I seriously discuss my wedding plans with him?

I picked up the card and read the message again.

My phone buzzed; it was a message from the Comedian:

He misses you and a picture of him on the bed, sheet covering to his waist and the outline of an extremely hard, thick dick pressing to be released.

I smiled.

I walked over, threw the card in the trash, and headed to bed.

I looked at the photo on my phone again, moving my fingers to my clit, and I closed my eyes and thought about how my entire body was electrified with The Comedian. I let myself get lost in remembering the pleasure of him on top of me.

My fingers played with the nub between my folds, and it did not take long until the climax of pleasure went through me again and then again.

I fell asleep with a smile on my face.

28

SHIFTING GEARS

At dinner the next night, I told the girls about the flowers.

"Did you throw them away?" Alex asked.

"That is really weird. How did he pick the same flowers?" Baley wondered.

"He's just dumb," Sally declared.

I had not thrown them away. I had instead decided to look at them for what they were: pretty flowers. They were some of my favorites, and like most women, I did not usually buy flowers for myself.

"I think he searched the words 'Goddess' and 'Flowers' together. I know because I did it this morning and they are the first flowers to pop up."

After a good night's sleep, I knew that I was not going to give any more energy to Jessie. He had already gotten more than his fair share.

"I don't want to talk about Jessie. I want to talk about The Comedian!" I said, feeling better just saying that out loud.

Over some warm lattes and a couple of desserts, I told them almost every detail of the night.

"That sounds amazing," Sally said, smiling.

Baley wanted me to come up with a new nickname for him, but I told her it was already in my phone and way too much effort to change at this point. This caused Sally to almost choke on her coffee from laughing.

Sitting with my friends and being able to safely share my adventures meant the world to me.

> *Whore Tip: You should always surround yourself with people that add to your life in some way. Even if it just being a safe person to talk to.*

My reaction to the Jessie thing told me that I still had not gotten myself to a place to consider opening myself up to something more than casual encounters.

Part of me fought with trying to go back to what I grew up considering a "normal" relationship. The fact is that you need to have the type of relationship that works for you mentally, emotionally, and physically. You shouldn't define yourself by what others want you to do. Be defined by what you want. If you are true to yourself, and choose the right supportive friends, then happiness is easy to find.

> *Whore Tip: Be true to you.*

My phone buzzed. "Is that the Magic Cock?" Baley asked.

"You really need to let that go." Alex smirked playfully.

I looked down at the text, and it was actually from Jordan, the super-hot Uber driver.

"Actually, remember Benedick?"

Sally's face scrunched up and she shook her head. "How have you not blocked his number?"

"Agreed," Baley chimed in.

Alex tilted her head. "You're still talking to him?"

"First, no, I am not still talking with him. Second, I don't need to block him. I have become an expert at ignoring texts, and third, this is the sexy Uber driver from that night." I showed them the text: *You up for a drive?*

"Yes!" Baley exclaimed.

Alex, Sally, and I just looked at her, narrowing our eyes.

"You seem super excited about this one," said Alex, taking another bite of one of the slices of cheesecake on the table.

"I am," Baley blurted out, "for Randi. I mean, she had some bad/weird luck there for a bit. Would be nice to see her have a good streak again. That is all. Well, that and he sounded yummy."

"He is yummy, well at least what I have seen of him. I will update you to the level of yumminess when we get to that point." I did not think it was an "if." I knew it would happen.

"However, my girl," I said, gesturing to my crotch, "needs a bit of downtime."

I texted him back, asking if he was free on Saturday. I knew he might be driving that night, so I was open for any time after I gave myself some rest.

He texted back: *Absolutely! What would you like to do?*

I pondered for a moment and decided that a drive sounded fun and texted him back. We set a date for an afternoon drive.

About an hour later, we finally decided to call it a night. I grabbed a new paranormal romance book on my way out and decided that the book and bottle of wine would be my company for tomorrow night.

Nothing like muscle bound, shapeshifting bad boys that always know the perfect thing to say to remind you that a healthy fantasy life is perfectly normal.

29

DINERS, DRIVE-INS, AND DICKS

I let myself sleep in on Saturday. I wasn't meeting Jordan, aka the Driver, my nickname for him, until the afternoon.

Since he drove for a living, I thought it might be fun to do the driving this time. He agreed and gave me his address. I picked him up in the afternoon, and we headed out.

When I got to his place, he walked out to meet me as I pulled into the driveway. He looked even better then I remembered. Wearing jeans and a snug t-shirt, he smiled and got in the car.

Before I could say anything, he leaned over and kissed me lightly on the lips.

"Wow...Um... Hi." My voice was breathy.

Smiling, he turned to put on his seatbelt. "So what adventure do you have in store for me?"

"Do you like coffee?"

"I kinda live off the stuff." His voice was huskier than I remembered.

"Then you will enjoy this."

I took him to a little drive-thru coffee shop on the beach. It was a local favorite, but they used coffee from Hawaii and the ice cubes were frozen coffee.

Grabbing the coffee, we headed to a parking lot near the beach. The parking lot was only a couple of feet from the sand, and if you got a good spot, you were basically looking out over the beach to the water.

Finding a great spot, I rolled the windows down, leaving the air conditioning blowing on our feet.

"This is nice," he said, taking a drink.

"Thank you. I aim to please," I winked, taking a sip of my own.

"Do you come here often?"

I laughed and then he said, "Wow. That was...I did not mean..."

"What? To say the cheesiest pick-up line ever?"

"That is not the cheesiest by far, my beautiful friend."

"Really? Please enlighten me then." I couldn't keep the smile from my lips.

He proceeded to hit me with the following:

"Would you grab my arm, so I can tell my friends I've been touched by an angel?"

"Kiss me if I'm wrong, but dinosaurs still exist, right?"

"Is your name Google? Because you have everything I've been searching for."

"There must be something wrong with my eyes. I can't take them off you."

"Are you my phone charger? Because without you, I'd die."

"Somebody call the cops because it's got to be illegal to look that good!"

His voice for each one added to the cheese factor, and I could not catch my breath I was laughing so hard.

Whore Tip: Even a bad pick-up line used the right way can get you a number or more.

"That was amazing," I told him when I recovered.

"Would it be cheesy to tell you that I think you have a really sexy smile?" he asked, his voice husky now.

"Yes," I replied. "But with that voice and those lips, you could say just about anything and melt my panties off."

For a moment, he held my gaze and then laughter burst from his lips.

When the laughter died down, I asked him if he wanted to walk on the sand for a bit. As we strolled, I went over what I was looking for.

I was surprised to find that he was almost half a foot taller than me when we got out of the car. I knew from the night we met that he was well defined, but it was even more so standing next to him. I could not wait to tell Baley how yummy I now found him.

Usually, I have the conversation over text or a messenger in an app. It was refreshing to have it in person, seeing the look in his eyes when I told him how truly casual I wanted this to be, that there was no way for this to "turn into something more."

As much as you would believe that most guys would be totally down for this type of relationship, I found that men, like women (and any other gender) do desire the emotional connection. Just a casual sex relationship does not work for most.

Most of the people I talk with can't have a one night stand. They want more, to create some kind of future. So my list of rules was important.

He told me that he had a couple of one-time encounters with women. He admitted that when he had them, one was not great in bed, and the one that was started stalking him after their encounter.

Jordan asked if anyone had ever broken the rules. Yes, a couple had, and a few more had not even gotten to round one because red flags told me they were not the right kind of person for this.

"Did I make this weird?" I finally asked, when he was quiet for a moment.

He shook his head. "Not weird. Just thinking. What you are proposing...it is just not something I expected."

We headed back toward the car. I could tell he was taking what I said seriously. Since I do not normally get to see this side of the process, it was just as interesting to me to watch.

As I unlocked the car and opened my door, he leaned onto the roof. "So, your..." I could tell he was trying to find the word.

"Playmate?" I offered up.

"Yes, playmate." I could tell by the way he said it that he wasn't comfortable with it yet, but he smiled as he continued, "They don't get jealous? Or ask about the other guys?"

"If they get jealous, then they are not someone for me. As far as asking about other guys, I have had some men that were turned on by it. But it usually doesn't come up. I like to focus on the enjoyment of the person I am with in that moment." I winked, getting in the car.

Whore Tip: Remember, not every person handles information the same way. Make sure you are willing to give someone the time they need.

On the drive back to his place, I turned on a playlist of what I called driving music, songs I loved and could sing along to when I was alone in the car or with friends. I decided not to bust out my singing voice for Jordan just yet.

The music filled the spaces of silence where I could tell he was thinking. When we arrived at his house, I put the car into park. He stared forward for a minute and then turned and said, "Not sure if you have already decided if you wanted to come inside, but I would like to invite you in."

I looked at his eyes, and he seemed nervous.

Instead of just responding with words, I turned off the car, undid my seatbelt, and got out, closing the door and heading to his front door.

He jumped out of the car and followed me, unlocking the door and showing me inside. Before the door closed, I locked my car.

Whore Tip: Actions can scream louder than words.

30

Going for a Ride

I took a few steps into the living room as the Driver closed the door. I looked around and there was a stack of books, some of them open on the table in the dining area. He was a student.

He put his keys down and pulled his phone out of his pocket.

I wanted to ask if he was nervous, but there are times when asking that question simply made the situation worse.

He finally walked up, leaned in, and kissed me.

At first it was gentle, but then like a switch was flipped, he claimed my mouth with his.

His tongue slid between his lips and caressed mine. I could still taste the coffee on him. His lips pressed harder as he sucked on my tongue, pulling me deeper into mouth.

Pulling back for a moment, he looked down, and there was a hunger in his eyes. Any reservations he might have had were gone.

"You're very yummy," my voice honeyed, "and I want to taste you."

He growled low in his throat, and in a quick motion lifted me off my feet and carried me to his bedroom.

When we entered the room, he set me on the bed. I watched as he removed his shirt, showing me all the lines of all the muscles on his chest and abs. I found myself wanting to trace down every line with my tongue.

Whore Tip: Stop and admire the beauty you see before you.

He slid his shoes off and unbuttoned his jeans, walking forward to stand in front of me. I could see the outline of his cock and slid my hand up to stroke it through the fabric. Pulling at the waist, I slid his pants and underwear down, so he sprang free.

Running my fingernails up his legs until I wrapped my hand around his shaft, I brought the tip to my lips. I slowly licked around the entire head, swirling it in my mouth as my hand stroked up and down his entire length.

With each motion, I took him deeper into my mouth until I felt him hit the back of my throat, then sucked hard, pulling him out. Hearing his breathing getting heavier and the noises of pleasure drove my need for him.

A few more strokes, and he placed his hand on my shoulder. "Stop. My god."

"You want me to stop?" I purred.

"Yes, but no. I don't want to cum yet," he said, pulling me up to my feet.

In a quick motion, he pulled my shirt over my head. He then knelt to undo and pull down my shorts and panties which I stepped out of. My flip-flops had fallen off on the way to bedroom.

As he cast the clothes away, he looked up at me, and I undid my bra, letting it fall to the floor as well.

His hands reached up to cup each breast, caressing them. "I am going to make you scream."

"Promise?" I replied.

His grin widened as he pushed me back on the bed. Opening my legs, he moved in, pushing my knees toward my chest.

Holding me in place, his tongue pressed against my core.

"God, you are so wet." His voice was hungry.

"I'm so ready," I sat up, causing him to rear back. I leaned in, licking my wetness off of his lips. He growled and opened the nightstand drawer.

As he slid the condom on, I moved back onto the bed on my side, facing away from him. Joining me in the bed, he nuzzled my neck as he pulled my nipple.

I lifted my leg, moving my hips, and he moved to slide inside me. I moaned as every inch slid inside.

Rocking my hips back to meet his thrust, I began to moan. He moved his fingertips to knead my core as he thrust harder.

Moaning louder, I held onto the bed, wanting more of him inside me.

"Say my name," he whispered into my ear. "Please baby, I am so close."

I moaned, "Cum for me Jordan!" and he did, hard.

He kissed my neck and shoulders and rolled onto his back, and I did the same.

"That was fucking amazing," he said after catching his breath and removing the used condom.

"Agreed."

I turned on my side to face him. "Ready for round two?"

He laughed, then rolled back to face me. "Absolutely yes!"

Whore Tip: Always ask for what you want.

The Driver and I got to play two more times before he had to get ready to drive.

As I drove home, I found myself needing to rest my cash-and-prizes again. This was a very nice problem to have.

31

BLURRED LINE

I was sitting on the couch in comfy clothes, cuddled under the blanket, sipping a hot tea, eating cookies, and watching one of my favorite movies. It was pure heaven.

I had texted Sally to let her know I was home safe. I also texted Baley to tell her how incredibly yummy the Driver really was. She called after receiving the text and forced me to give her details. She couldn't wait, and her giddiness made me laugh.

At times, the girls would champion one of my conquests. Everyone has a type and in some of the playmates, my friends got to live vicariously through my adventures.

> *Whore Tip: It is okay to imagine yourself in another life from time to time, as long as you are super happy going back to your own world.*

There was a knock at the door. I paused the movie and went to the door, expecting it to be a package drop off. When I opened the door, it was Jessie.

Fuck!

"What are you doing here?" My tone was not welcoming.

"I need to talk to you."

"I doubt that."

"Seriously. Can I come in?"

I debated telling him no, but at the same time, I did not want to deal with my neighbors watching me argue with him on my front porch.

I stepped back and gestured for him to come in.

As he walked inside, he looked nervous or distressed. I couldn't tell which. I also did not care.

"What are you doing here?"

"Did you get the flowers?"

I glared at him. "You know the answer to that."

He shrugged.

"You didn't say anything."

Part of me wanted to tell him all the reasons why I did not say anything to him about the flowers, but it wasn't worth it.

"Jessie," I said in the calmest voice I could muster, "what are you doing here?"

He met my gaze for the first time, which was weird. Here was this larger than life soldier-type acting like a child being scolded.

"I am getting a divorce," he finally said with a sigh. "I wanted you to know."

Before blurting out the first things that came to mind, I took a deep breath.

Whore Tip: Take a breath when emotions are crazy.
That way you get the chance to think out your answer.

"Okay." I decided to keep it simple.

"I came here tonight," he began, "I came because I want to fix this."

This was not how I wanted to end this night.

Sitting on one side of the couch just in case he wanted to sit on the other, I took another sip of my tea to give myself a moment to figure out how I wanted this to go.

"Jessie," I started, "I need to be clear about something. So please really listen to me."

He nodded and sat on the other side of the couch.

Looking at him, it was hard for me not to remember all of the amazing times we had playing together. His blue eyes searched my face for signals. I took a deep breath and continued.

"There is a part of me that wants to tell you what I had to deal with after you came clean." He started to speak, but I held my hand up. "Let me finish."

Nodding his head again, he was silent.

"I, instead, need you to understand that even if you are getting a divorce, it doesn't change that you broke my trust," I paused to let my words sink in, "and there is nothing you can do to repair that. Nothing."

He looked down at his hands instead of meeting my gaze.

> *Whore Tip: Truly evaluate if you can repair a betrayal.*
> *If you cannot, then do not add stress to your life trying*
> *to make it "work" for the person who betrayed you.*

We sat on the couch for several minutes in silence. I drank some more of my tea and gave him the time he needed to, hopefully, accept what I had said.

Finally, he stood up slowly, and I joined him.

"I understand," he said, although I do not know if he believed it one hundred percent.

He began to walk toward the door, and as he opened it, he turned to face me. "I want you to know how sorry I am for not telling you the truth to begin with. But I did not want my life without you in it."

I nodded at him. "Thank you, Jessie."

There was so much more that I wanted to say or possibly even lecture him on. None if it would change the outcome I needed, which was for him to walk out of my life.

Whore Tip: Be willing to close the door so the other person can walk away. Because if you leave it open even a smidge, they might try to come back through.

He pulled a small box out of his jacket and set it on the table near the couch, and left, closing the door behind him.

I let out a breath that I did not know I was holding as I walked over to pick up the small box. Part of me wanted to be able to simply throw it away like you sometimes see people do in the movies. I was not one of those people that could do that.

I opened it, hoping it wasn't an engagement ring, which was my first thought, which in itself was weird.

Luckily, that wasn't what it was. It was a small hand-carved watusi cow figurine made of some kind of dark wood.

I smiled a little, went to the bedroom, and put this on a small shelf on my dresser.

This I would keep, reminding me to make sure to never let myself get into a situation like this one again. I would know where the line was between playmate and something else, a line that got blurry with Jessie. I needed to keep that line crystal clear.

Whore Tip: Learn from your mistakes by acknowledging what caused you to make them to begin with and fixing that. It is not your job to fix the part another person played in it.

32

SNAKES IN A BASKET

I did end up telling Alex and only Alex about the interaction that I had with Jessie. She was proud of how I handled it. Even if she would have thrown the gift away, she understood why I kept it.

She also ended up calling me up on a Saturday to come over to her house urgently. She said that she had a company putting in a deck and that a snake had gotten into the house.

"You need to come right now!" Her voice super panicked.

"A snake? In your house? Where is Aaron?" I figured this was the perfect type of thing a husband was supposed to handle.

"He is traveling. Just come now. I think it is an anaconda!"

"You think it's an anaconda?"

She just whimpered, and I imagined she was standing on a chair surrounded by a giant snake like in a terribly written nineties horror movie. "I'm on my way," I finally said, grabbed my keys, and headed out.

> *Whore Tip: Always help a friend in need. Even if the request is ridiculous.*

It took me about twenty minutes to get to her house. I ended up parking down the street because of the work trucks out in front.

I opened the door to find Alex standing waiting for me. She pointed to the kitchen. "It is in there."

Walking in the kitchen, I was expecting to find a snake over ten feet long, as thick as a log, coiled and waiting to swallow me whole.

Instead, there was a small rectangular basket upside-down on the floor with a couple of phone books stacked on top.

I leaned out of the kitchen. "First, where did you find phone books? And is the snake in the basket?"

She glared at me. "Yes. I hit it with a broom." I noticed she was still holding the broom. Alex's kitchen lead to the dining room, which had a sliding glass door. I walked over to the door and saw that there were a couple of guys working on putting in a deck out back. One of contractors was facing away from me, using his hammer shirtless. It was a nice distraction.

"Randi!" she yelled. I turned back into the kitchen and decided to find out exactly what we were dealing with.

Positioning myself in front of the basket, I removed the phone books and then grabbed the basket, jumping back just in case it was coiled to strike.

There on the floor was small black snake. It was about two feet long and as thick around as a dime. It also appeared to not be moving.

I looked around for a dustpan and scooped it up, intending to throw it into the yard.

"Want some help?" the voice started me, so I dropped the snake off the dustpan. This made the shirtless man in front of me chuckle.

It occurred to me what I must look like. I ran out of the house in the comfy shorts and tank top I had been wearing when Alex called.

"This is a fierce creature," I gestured at the dead snake. "You sure you can handle it?"

He simply smiled, "I will try. After all, it isn't often you get to save a damsel in distress." He leaned down and picked up the snake in his gloved hands and turned to take the body outside.

"Thank you," I called after him and turned back to Alex.

"The beast has been slain," I told her, making a grandiose gesture and bowing.

She crinkled her nose. "You killed it?"

"No," I said, but now she looked confused. "You killed it. I just assisted in its removal from the kitchen."

"Assisted?" she said, putting the broom down.

I went to sit on the couch "Yep, assisted. I had the help of one of your super-hot shirtless construction workers."

She came and sat next to me. "Thank you."

"No problem." I patted her leg. "Sooo... whatcha building out there?"

"A deck. Aaron's idea to enjoy more outside time." Alex didn't seem thrilled with her husband's idea of an enjoyable time.

"Well at least you have a pleasant view during the building process."

"His name is Don," she said, smiling.

"Would it be weird giving him my number?"

"Is any one of these acquisitions not weird?"

"True. Hand me a pen."

I quickly jotted a note down and handed it to her to give to him when he was heading out.

It simply said: *To my hero, let me buy you a drink.* I included my number.

Whore Tip: You will never get what you don't ask for.

33

Don Juan – Not Really

on called me that night. This surprised me since most people texted. Because I did not know the number, it went to voicemail.

"Heya. You left the note without a name. So, since I don't know what your name is, I will call you Sweetness, and yes, I would love that drink." His voice was deep and husky.

I was excited to think about his broad chest, thick arms, and that he looked like he could hold me against a wall the entire time he pounded me.

I texted him: *How does tomorrow night sound? 7pm at Brew Bus?*

It was a local craft beer bar that I did not frequent much. This made it easy to avoid if a situation did not work out.

> *Whore Tip: Always have a Plan B. Sometimes an actual plan and sometimes the pill, just in case.*

He texted back right away: *CU@7.*

Looking at the text, I was irked. It is a pet peeve when people shorten every word in a text. I brushed it off, however, and looked forward to our meeting.

When I arrived, he was already waiting for me outside with two beers at one of the high-top tables. He had his shirt on now and shorts.

"Hi, Sweetness," he said as I approached.

"Hi," I smiled. "It's Randi."

Getting a better look at him, I noticed he had a little grey mixed in with his brown. He had a deep tan, most likely from working in the sun shirtless.

"I got you a chocolate porter, Sweetness," he said with a wink. "I hope you like the taste." This time his eyes scanned up and down my body, lingering on my breasts for a couple seconds too long before he met my gaze again.

It was uncomfortable instead of alluring.

I picked up the beer, about to take a sip, and then I looked down. It was open. "I'll be right back."

Before he could say or do anything, I walked up to the bar and got three more bottles, asking the bartender to pour mine out. I told him there was a bug in it.

I brought the bottles out, placing them on the table. "I said I was buying you a drink."

I sat on one of the stools, taking a sip of the new bottle I brought out. The flavor was called Basic B!tch: It was a pumpkin spice milk stout. It was my favorite, which I would have told him if he asked.

"So, Sweetness," he leaned in, putting his hand on my thigh, "what do you do?"

"Do?" I asked, taking another drink.

"Like for fun," he said, winking again.

In case you were wondering, I was up to about ten Red Flags right now.

Whore Tip: Always, always, always trust your gut.

I debated how to get out of this situation. Not out of fear. This was creepy, not scary. It just had been a while since I met someone and had this reaction.

He had been gorgeous at the house, and now he had the "Hey baby" vibe of a guy who hit on every woman at the bar until someone said yes.

"So, do you like getting your hands dirty?" he asked, flexing a little as he picked up his beer.

I pulled out my phone quickly and looked at the screen. "Crap," I said. "Give me a minute."

I walked away from the table toward the edge of the patio area talking into the phone low enough volume he couldn't make out my words but the tone, which of course was worried and concerned.

Then, looking exasperated, I hung it up and walked back over to the table.

"I have to go." I slid the phone in my pocket. "That was work. Raincheck?"

"Work?"

"Yeah, real big project due and there is some kind of issue with the files. I have to head in to work it out." I mustered my best annoyed face.

"Sweetness, I had such a night planned for us." He did a pouty face then.

"Aww, I am sorry. Maybe I can text when I am done and see if we can pick up where this left off?" I tried to sound interested.

Standing up, he moved to take my hand. He kissed it. "Until tonight."

I pulled my hand back and waved, heading out. As I walked to my car, making sure he wasn't following me, I knew I could have been way more direct. I could have just stormed out or tried to make a point about being creepy. That would have just end resulted in him trying to "fix it." That was something I knew I didn't want.

I called Alex on the way home to tell her what happened and to apologize if he still had work to do at the house. She wasn't worried. Her husband would be home in the morning, and she would leave him to deal with Don and the amazing deck.

34

SIMPLE PLEASURES IN LIFE

When I got home, I took a shower. Sometimes you just need to wash off an experience.

Looking at my phone, I had three missed calls and six texts all from Don. I blocked his number. This feature on the phone is one of the best ever.

My phone chimed with a new text: *What are you doing right now?*

It was the Comedian.

I replied: *What am I doing? Or who should I be doing?*

His response was quick: *Yes! Come over?*

As was mine: *Be there in 20.*

It threw on jeans, no undies as they were coming off anyway, a bra, and t-shirt. I put on some mascara and grabbed my keys.

When I got to his door and knocked, he yelled for me to come inside. I walked in and he was leaning on the doorframe of the bedroom, his massively hard cock in his hand as he stroked it.

"Sorry to keep you waiting," I mused as I put my keys down on the counter. Walking toward him, I pulled my clothes off, dropping them on the floor as he continued to masturbate.

As I got close, I leaned in and took over for him, rubbing his length and kissing his neck up to his ear, nibbling on the lobe.

He slid his now free fingertips through my wet pussy lips.

Goosebumps blossomed on my skin; my pulse began to race as I moved my free hand to hold on to his shoulder.

Heat spread from my core as I came, breathy moans escaping my lips, and I felt my release.

His eyes sparkled with desire. He leaned in thrusting his tongue in my mouth, chasing mine with his. He tasted like root beer, and it made me smile as he pulled his head back.

"What?" he prodded.

"You taste like sweetness."

We moved into the bedroom. He pulled me with him until we reached the edge of bed. He purred, "I want to see if you taste like sweetness."

He lay on the bed, but as I moved to join him, he shook his head. "I want you right here," he said, gesturing to his lips.

Biting my lip, I moved to comply, placing a knee on either side of his head and facing down the length of his body.

His hands moved to guide me into his mouth, sucking my clit into his mouth and then using his tongue to flick against it, driving me to the edge, and then I spilled over into ecstasy.

As I came again, my hand cupped his shaft, and with equal hunger, I took his head into my mouth. His suction released as my lips slid farther down his shaft. His girth made it impossible for me to take him into my mouth too far. My mouth simply wasn't big enough. So, I decided to approach this like a large swirl cone that was melting on all sides.

I licked, sucked, and stroked every inch of him in unison with his mouth on my body. Letting my teeth lightly graze his head, I sucked as much of him in my mouth as possible. Moans escaped his lips as goosebumps puckered on his skin, driving me harder. I wanted him to feel what he made me feel. As I pushed myself to take more and more with each mouthful, he growled, "I'm cumming...!" and I felt him pulse as he exploded in my mouth.

When his spasms finished, I moved to lay beside him, putting my head on his chest.

"That was fucking amazing," he breathed.

"I agree."

We laid for a while with him just lightly caressing my back with his hand and my eyes closed in contentment. Then we moved, rolling over to open the drawer to the nightstand and grabbing a condom. As he rolled to face me again, I could see his cock was once again standing at attention.

"Ready for round two?"

I was!

35

Finding My Happy Place

I t has been three months since Jessie had walked out the door. Every now and then, I looked at that watusi, and it did what I hoped it would: reminded me to stay true to what I really wanted from my playmates.

Although I again had a few that I could have fun with when I wanted, I made sure to remember where the line was emotionally. If I felt myself coming close to crossing it again, I would take some me time.

I found that these types of relationships, or encounters, were not set up to be long term arrangements. They were instead best if you gave them a little time and distance.

On a side note, it turned out that Alex did not actually kill the snake. It was just knocked a little silly by her broom and made a full recovery. Well, at least she thinks it is the same snake.

Whore Tip: Remember only you can create your happy place. Even if other people stop by to visit every now and then.

Coming Soon:

Ever wonder what Randi was like as she began her sexual exploration? Find out in *The Training of the Tramp* coming in the fall of 2021!

ABOUT THE AUTHOR

So here is something about little ole me; I have had a very interesting upbringing, starting with growing up in Hollywood, CA. Never shy, I learned that if you are not willing to try something new, you may let life simply pass you by. I love meeting people from all walks of life and these experiences inspire me on a daily basis. As a true friend once pointed out "You are never a complete waste, you can always be used as a bad example." So, what's the worst that can happen?

www.DaliaLance.com
Twitter: @DaliaLance
Facebook.com/authordalialance

Never miss another Whore Tip!

Discover more at
4HorsemenPublications.com

10% off using HORSEMEN10

www.ingramcontent.com/pod-product-compliance
Lightning Source LLC
Chambersburg PA
CBHW050141110726
47898CB00008B/2616